Henry Ford

Young Man with Ideas

Illustrated by Wallace Wood

Henry Ford

Young Man with Ideas

By Hazel B. Aird
and
Catherine Ruddiman

Aladdin Paperbacks

First Aladdin Paperbacks edition 1986
Copyright © 1960 by the Bobbs-Merrill Company, Inc.

ALADDIN PAPERBACKS
An imprint of Simon & Schuster Children's Publishing Division
1230 Avenue of the Americas, New York, NY 10020

Manufactured in the United States of America
28 30 29

Library of Congress Cataloging-in-Publication Data
Aird, Hazel B.
  Henry Ford, young man with ideas

Reprint of the ed.: Indianapolis : Bobbs-Merrill, 1984, c1960.
  Published 1960 under title: Henry Ford, boy with ideas.
  Summary: the early life of the American automotive industrialist who founded the Ford Motor Company and pioneered in assembly-line methods of mass production.
  1. Ford, Henry, 1863-1947—Juvenile literature.
  2. Ford Motor Company—History—Juvenile literature. 3. Automobile industry and trade—United States—History—Juvenile literature.
  4. Industrialists—United States—Biography—Juvenile literature.
  [1. Ford, Henry, 1863-1947. 2. Businessmen 3. Ford Motor Company.
  4. Automobile industry and trade—Biography] I. Ruddiman, Catherine.
II. Wood, Wallace, ill. III. Title.
HD9710.U54F533 1986 338.7′6292′0924 [B] [92] 86-10756
          ISBN-13: 978-0-02-041910-5 (Aladdin pbk.)
          ISBN-10: 0-02-041910-4 (Aladdin pbk.)
                    0315 OFF

To my mother,
Margaret Ford Ruddiman,
who shared the hopes and dreams
of her brother Henry Ford
with sympathy and understanding

Catherine Ruddiman

To my two nephews,
Peter Bradshaw and Peter LaRoche,
in memory of their grandfather,
Peter Blair

Hazel Blair Aird

Many incidents in this book are based on "Memories of My Brother Henry Ford" by Margaret Ford Ruddiman, published in the September, 1953 issue of Michigan History, by the Michigan Historical Commission.

Illustrations

Full pages

Numerous smaller illustrations

Contents

CHILDHOOD
OF FAMOUS
AMERICANS

★ ★ # Henry Ford

Young Man with Ideas

A Teakettle
and a Clock

"HENRY! Henry Ford! You come away from that teakettle this instant!"

Henry jumped and pulled his hand away. "But Mama, I'm just trying to hold the lid down, that's all. It keeps jumping up and down."

"Yes, and you're just trying to scald your hand, too," Mrs. Ford said.

"What makes the lid jump up and down that way?" Henry asked eagerly.

"If I knew, I would tell you, son. It just does. That's all I know. But if you don't stop asking questions, young man, I'll—well, I don't know what I'll do with you."

11

Henry knew he would have to do something worse than ask questions for his mother to punish him. But maybe he should stay away from the cookstove and not bother her any more.

"Now run along out of my way," she went on. "Your grandmother and I have to cook dinner for two extra hands today. The men are cutting the wheat. It will be noon before we know it."

"That's when both hands stand straight up, isn't it, Mama?" Henry asked. "That's when it's noon, isn't it?"

"Yes, that's right," his mother answered patiently.

Henry looked at the clock that was standing on the shelf over the sink. He saw that the long hand stood straight up and the short hand pointed straight down.

"What time is it now, Mama?" he asked.

"It's six o'clock. The sun's been up almost an hour. I must teach you to tell time. That will be one less question you will have to ask me. We'll have a lesson after supper. How would you like that?"

Henry knew that he would like that. It always was fun when his mother had what she called "a lesson" in the evening. He called it "playing school."

Standing on his toes, he tried to see over the picture that was painted in bright colors on the

lower half of the clock. Suddenly he noticed that the long hand gave a tiny jerk, then another one and another one. It wasn't long before the long hand had moved to the number one on the face of the clock.

Henry tiptoed over to his mother, who was kneading bread at the table. He pulled gently on the sleeve of her flowered calico dress. "Mama, please may I ask one more question?" he asked.

"Of course, Henry," she answered with a smile. "I just hope I can answer it. You do ask such strange questions sometimes."

"What makes the hands on the clock move?"

Mrs. Ford looked down at her son's serious face. She wiped the flour from her hands and knelt down to take his hands in her own.

"Henry, I don't mean to be cross about your asking questions. I'm always sorry when I can't answer them. But you ask so many questions

14

for a little boy! You must learn to be patient.
Perhaps some day you can find the answers to
all your questions yourself.

"Then maybe people will say, 'Henry Ford
knows what makes the teakettle lid dance. Henry Ford knows what makes a clock run. Henry
Ford knows just about everything.'"

Henry squeezed his mother's arm and they
both laughed.

"Now run along," she said. "You can watch
the men run the McCormick reaper from the
window over there."

A few moments later, as Henry stood at the
window, he heard his mother say to Grandma
O'Hern, "That boy! He can ask more questions
than you can shake a stick at."

"You know the old saying, Mary," his grandmother answered. " 'Curiosity killed a cat. Satisfaction brought it back.'"

Mrs. Ford laughed softly. "If there's any

truth in that saying, my oldest son certainly is going to find a lot of satisfaction in life."

Henry was puzzled. He didn't exactly know what his grandmother's words meant. "I'm not a cat," he thought. Still, he liked the way the words rhymed.

From the window he could see the team of dappled gray horses straining to pull the heavy reaper over the wheat field. He knew that Mike, the hired man, was driving the team. He could see him slapping the reins over their backs, urging them on, and could hear his cheerful voice calling, "Wh-upp, wh-upp, wh-upp!"

Henry smiled to himself. He had just thought of something funny. "I guess I would rather be a cat than a horse," he thought. "A horse has to work too hard."

He could see his father and Grandfather O'Hern walking beside the reaper, raking wheat from the platform. Mr. Ruddiman and Mr. Les-

16

lie, two neighbors who lived in the Scotch Settlement near by, were gathering the wheat into bundles.

"Mama, come look!" Henry cried suddenly. "There are puddles of water all over the field."

"Why, we haven't had rain for weeks," Mrs. Ford said, surprised. She came to the window to look out. "Those aren't puddles of water, Henry. You're seeing a mirage."

"What's a mirage?"

"It's a kind of trick the heat and light play when the weather's hot. Now don't ask me how it works. I don't know. All I know is that it means we're going to have another hot day."

"People think it never gets very hot in Michigan," his grandmother said. "It was almost a hundred in the shade the day Henry was born. Do you remember, Mary?"

Mrs. Ford laughed her tinkling laugh. "Yes, indeed, I remember, Mother. I sat under the willow tree in the front yard almost all day, fanning myself with a bunch of corn husks tied together for a fan."

Henry looked at his mother in surprise. He couldn't imagine her sitting down in the middle of the day. It was only in the evening after the kerosene lamps were lighted that he had ever seen her resting.

"Mama, my birthday's soon, isn't it? When is

it? I hope I get a wagon for my birthday. I can haul in the kindling wood with it," Henry said almost in one breath. "When is my birthday, Mama?"

"Well, let's see now." His mother put her hand up to her head and pretended she couldn't quite remember. She turned to Grandma. "Do you remember when Henry's birthday is, Mother? I don't."

"Well, now, let me think. I think it's next Friday—no, I think maybe it's Thursday——"

"Oh!" Henry stamped his foot. "You're both teasing me. Tell me! You remember when I was born!"

"Yes, Henry, I do remember," Mrs. Ford said. "It's a day I'll never forget, July 30, 1863. That will make you five years old next Thursday. You're getting to be a big boy."

"I'm big enough to haul in the heavy pieces of wood—that is, if I had a wagon."

"Well, while you're waiting for a wagon you can get me some apples," his mother said, laughing. "Pick up the windfalls from under the trees, Henry. I'll make a couple of apple pies."

"Now if I had a wagon——"

"Yes, yes, I know. If you had a wagon. Next thing I know you'll be wanting a team to pull it. Fill a basket full of apples and be sure you pick the best ones."

"The best ones are still on the tree," Henry said. "May I climb the tree?"

"No, no, the windfalls are good enough for pies. I remember a verse I used to say when I was a little girl.

'The apple grows so bright and high
　　And ends its day in apple pie.'

Now run along and get the apples."

"Oh, I like that," Henry said. He skipped out the back door to the orchard. As he filled his basket with apples he recited the verse over and over again.

Within five minutes or even less he had forgotten the apples. He had thought of another question that he wanted to ask. This time he would ask his father. He would have to run fast to the wheat field before he forgot it.

Mechanical Experiment

"It's so quiet in here you could hear a pin drop," said Mrs. Ford.

The Ford family was gathered around the fireplace in the sitting room one cool, early fall evening.

"Where's Henry?" asked Mr. Ford, glancing over the top of his newspaper. "You usually know when he's around. He chatters away like a magpie."

Without answering, Mrs. Ford pointed to the round table in the center of the room. Beneath the fringed tablecloth she could see a pair of shoe soles, toes down. She knew that Henry was wearing those shoes and that he was lying on his stomach.

"I wonder what he's up to?" she whispered.

"You can be sure it has something to do with nuts, bolts, and screws," Mr. Ford said. "I never saw a boy take to such things as he does."

"You should see how much he can cram into one pocket," Mrs. Ford said with a twinkle in her eye. "I told him the other day he had everything in there but a plow and a harrow."

Under the table Henry smiled. "I hope John doesn't look under here to see what I'm doing," he thought.

It was hardly likely that John would. He was sitting in a chair with his legs crossed, just as his father was, and pretending to read a newspaper several days old.

As Mrs. Ford said, the room was quiet and peaceful. The click of her knitting needles reminded Henry of the click-click of a hay rake.

The crackle of logs in the fire almost covered the sound of the wind whistling around the corners of the house. Near the table Margaret was carefully building blocks into a tall pile. Jane, the baby, was fast asleep in her cradle close to the hearth.

Suddenly a wheel came rolling out from under the table, and Henry came after it on his hands and knees. Everyone looked up to watch the wheel circle around the room, out of Henry's reach. The faster he scrambled, the faster the wheel rolled in smaller and smaller circles. Just as he thought he had it, he lost his balance and Margaret's blocks came tumbling down in a heap. Henry sprawled full length on the floor.

The runaway wheel came to a stop on the toe of John's shoe. John looked down. "That's mine!" he shouted. "Mama! Henry's broken my butterfly!" He started to cry and Margaret, still more excited, started to jump up and down.

"He broke it! He broke it!" she cried. "Mama, Henry broke it!"

The noise awakened the baby and she started to cry, too. There was nothing quiet about the room now.

"Henry! John! Margaret! Sit down!" Mr. Ford's big voice could be heard above all the shouting and crying.

The children sat down at once. They knew their father meant what he said.

"Now tell me what this is all about," he said sternly. "John?"

"Henry broke my butterfly. He took all the wheels off and now it won't work," John sobbed.

"Stop your sniffling, John. You're too big to be crying. What about this, Henry? What do you have to say for yourself? Is that wheel part of John's toy?"

Henry hung his head. He looked under the table, where John's four-wheeled toy lay in several pieces. "Father, I just wanted to find out what made it work. I'll put it together again. Honest I will."

"Are you sure you can?" Mr. Ford asked.

"Oh, yes," Henry said quickly. "I was taking the wheels off when one got away from me." He looked at his father's stern face and added, "It won't be hard to fix. You see, when the wheels turn, the butterfly jumps up and down and the bell starts——"

"Never mind that now, Henry. You had no right to take John's toy apart. Put it on the table and go up to bed."

"Yes, Father," Henry said meekly.

"John, you go to bed, too," Mr. Ford said.

Henry and John trudged up the stairs. John was angry. "See what you've done, Henry," he said. "We get punished because of something you did. And you've broken my toy."

"I'm sorry, John," Henry said. "I'll fix it tomorrow. I know just how to put it together again so it will work."

"I hope you do," John said angrily.

Once they were in bed, John fell asleep almost at once, but Henry lay awake for a long time. He was thinking about the butterfly that jumped and the bell that chimed when the toy's wheels turned. After a while he heard his father bank the fire in the fireplace and knew that his parents and grandparents had gone to their bedrooms downstairs.

Slipping out of his bed, he tiptoed across the room and stood at the top of the stairs, listening. Except for his grandfather's muffled snore, the house was quiet. He crept slowly downstairs, remembering to miss the third step from the top because it squeaked.

A bright streak of flame danced in one corner of the fireplace. Henry gathered up the pieces of the toy and sat before the fireplace.

There was just enough light for him to finish putting the toy together.

He didn't hear his mother come into the room. "Henry," she said softly, "I thought you had gone to bed."

"Mama, I just had to see if I could put John's butterfly back together."

Mrs. Ford ruffled Henry's curly chestnut hair. "I guess I shouldn't scold you for being persistent," she said. "I'll sit here with you until you finish it."

"Thank you, Mama. I won't be long."

The Big Secret

HENRY could see his breath in the cold bedroom when he awakened one winter morning. He pulled the quilt up around his chin.

"I'll dress under the covers where it's warm," he thought. "Then I'll run lickety-split down to the kitchen."

He cautiously took one arm out from under the covers and felt around on the floor. He found his heavy wool stockings right where he had left them the night before.

"I'm glad Grandma taught me how to fold the foot in first," he thought. "It's easy to put stockings on once you get the foot in."

He squirmed under the covers. It wasn't easy to pull long stockings over long underwear. Without coming altogether out from under the covers, he put on his wool shirt and knickers.

"Henry, quit pulling the covers off," John said sleepily.

"Come on, sleepyhead," Henry said, yanking the top quilt off the bed. "It's time to get up. I heard Father and Grandpa leave a long time ago. They're cutting the big trees into cordwood today."

"Oh, maybe they'd let me help!" John jumped quickly out of bed. "Do you think they would, Henry? Are you going, too?"

"You know I have to shell corn, feed the chickens, and keep the woodbox filled. Mama's going to need lots of wood today. It's ironing day and it takes lots of wood to heat those flatirons."

"I know she's ironing today," John said crossly. "It's Tuesday, isn't it?"

Each day had its proper work in the Ford household.

> Wash on Monday.
> Iron on Tuesday.
> Mend on Wednesday.
> Churn on Thursday.
> Clean on Friday.
> Bake on Saturday.
> Rest on Sunday.

Henry didn't answer. He was sitting on the floor lacing his shoes. He tied and untied the laces several times.

"Say, aren't you dressed yet?" Henry finally asked. "Why don't you go downstairs? I can smell something awfully good."

John looked at him suspiciously. "What about you? Are you trying to get rid of me?"

"Well, if you *must* know," Henry said, rolling over on his stomach. He reached under the bed and pulled out a wooden box.

"What's that? What's in there?" John asked excitedly.

"It's a big secret. Promise you won't tell Father until I'm sure it will work. Promise?"

"Oh, yes, Henry, I promise," John said. "What's that hinge for? What are you going to do with that spring?" He looked in wonder at

the box filled with nuts, bolts, wire, and rods. "Where did you get all this stuff?"

"I found it in the tool shed," Henry answered. "I'm going to make something. I'll show you after a while."

The boys ran pell-mell down the stairs, around the hall and into the bright, warm kitchen.

"Good morning!" they shouted.

"Good morning, boys," their mother answered. "My goodness, you two are as frisky as the horses were when Mike took them out of the barn this morning." She smiled at them.

"Good morning, Grandma," Henry said, going up to his grandmother. Mrs. O'Hern was sitting at the spinning wheel close to the hearth, where it was warm.

"Good morning," she answered. "Sakes alive, Henry, seems as if every time I look at you, you have grown a foot. You're outgrowing your clothes so fast I'll have to keep the great wheel spinning all the time. You're going to be tall like your father."

The "great wheel," which was used for spinning wool, stood in one corner of the kitchen. Mrs. O'Hern was using the "little wheel" now to spin flax. It had a treadle, a kind of pedal which she worked up and down with her foot to keep the wheel turning.

Henry watched her foot closely as it moved up and down on the treadle. The wheel turned round and round, but the spindle which wound the flax went even faster.

"Your breakfast is on the table, boys, but wash up first," said Mrs. Ford.

She lifted Jane into her high chair. Margaret climbed proudly on a chair to sit beside Henry.

"Mama," John said eagerly, "may I go to the wood lot? I can help Father and Mike. I'll bet I can handle one end of that crosscut saw all by myself. May I go, Mama? May I?"

His mother smiled. "What would you do, ride on the saw like a teeter-totter?"

"Why do you want to go out there?" Henry asked. "Don't you want to help me?"

John remembered the box upstairs under the bed. He was curious to know what Henry would do with all those things. He decided to stay home and find out.

"There's enough wood in the woodbox to do until you finish your breakfast, Henry," Mrs. Ford said. "But it will have to be filled several times today, so don't go far away. I'll be glad when this ironing is done. I think I dislike ironing more than anything else I do. When you dislike doing something, though, it's best to do it right off."

"That's why I'm going to shell the corn first," Henry said. "I just don't like turning that wheel by hand. It seems to take forever to get half a pail full."

"There are no two ways about it, Henry, you'll never get anything done if you don't stop staring at that spinning wheel," his mother said. "A person would think you never had seen a spinning wheel before."

Soon they finished their breakfast. Henry and John put on their heavy coats, pulled stocking caps over their ears and woolen mittens on their hands, then went out to the cold, snow-covered yard. It wasn't long before they had a sled piled high with cordwood for the stove.

"John, you take the sled up to the house," Henry said. He put one last armful of wood on the sled. "Will you do that?"

"When are you going to work on your secret, Henry?" John asked.

"If you feed the chickens for me I can get at it right away," Henry said.

John kicked the snow with his foot. "You're always getting me to do your chores."

"I tell you what I'll do. If you feed the chickens for me I'll let you use my new skates. We'll go down to Roulo Creek this afternoon and I'll show you how to make a figure eight."

"Oh, all right," John said. "I hope I can make a figure eight as well as you can." He trudged off toward the house, pulling the sled.

"John," Henry called after him. "Will you get the box from under the bed for me? I'll be out in the shed."

"Oh, all right," John answered. "After I feed the chickens."

When John returned with the box some time later, he found Henry sitting on the floor in the shed. The corn sheller was on the floor beside him and in his hands he held the handle. He had taken it from the shaft of the sheller.

"Oh, Henry!" John cried. "Now you've done it! You'll get it from Father when he finds out you've broken the sheller."

Henry went on working without a word. He took one thing and then another from the box that John had brought him. After watching for a while, John wandered away. Henry was so busy he didn't even notice when John left.

"All I hope," he said to himself, "is that I get this finished before Father and Grandpa come in for dinner."

Time flew by. Henry found a use for every piece of material in his box. He wired the rod to the wheel shaft. He made a treadle by fastening two pieces of wood together with a hinge. He put the spring under the treadle so that it would spring back when he pushed down on it with his foot.

"Now what can I fasten the corn sheller to?" he wondered. "I don't want it to slip."

He saw the wooden box that had held his secret all night. "That's just the right height if I can stand it up on end," he said to himself.

So absorbed was he in his work that he did not hear the shed door open.

"Henry," his father said loudly, "didn't you hear your mother call you to fill the woodbox?"

"Oh!" Henry jumped. "I'm sorry, Father. I didn't hear her. Look here, Father! See what I've made!"

He put an ear of corn in the sheller. Then he pressed the treadle with his foot and the wheels inside the sheller began to turn. Teeth tore the kernels of corn from the cob and they dropped into a bucket on the floor.

Mr. Ford stared at Henry's handiwork. "Well, I'll be hornswoggled!" he exclaimed. "It runs just like a spinning wheel."

Henry beamed with pleasure. "It's easier than shelling corn by hand, too," he said.

Mr. Ford threw back his head and laughed. "I'll say one thing for you, son. If there's an easier way to do anything, you'll find it."

A Fool's Name–a Fool's Fame

ONE DAY Mr. Ford and Mike took a load of cordwood in to one of the machine shops in Detroit. Henry was in the yard when they returned.

"Henry, I brought a present for you from Detroit," Mr. Ford called from the wagon.

Henry ran to meet the wagon. "What is it?" he cried. "Is it peppermint candy? Is it the round red and white kind?"

"No, it's something that will last a lot longer than candy."

Mr. Ford jumped down from the wagon and let Mike take the team to the barn. He handed Henry a flat package wrapped in brown paper.

Henry shook the package, but it didn't rattle. Breaking the string impatiently, he tore off the paper and discovered a brand-new slate. Red and white cord resembling a stick of peppermint candy was wrapped around the outside of the wooden frame. A slate pencil was fastened to the frame with a cord.

Henry was delighted. "Oh, Father, I'm going to school!" he cried.

"Yes, you start Monday in the Scotch Settlement School. You're over seven now and it's time for you to start the winter term. I talked to Miss Nardin, the teacher, yesterday. I told her you knew your letters and numbers and could read some. She's expecting a smart pupil, son, so don't disappoint her."

Henry was glad he was going to the Scotch Settlement School. That was where his mother had gone when she was a girl.

Monday morning Henry left home bright and

early, carrying his new slate and a tin lunch pail that Mike had given him. He followed Roulo Creek part of the way. But he was so eager to get to school that he had no time to look for rabbits or birds, as he usually did. When he reached the road that led to the school, he ran and skipped the rest of the way.

Miss Nardin called the class to order.

"We have two new pupils this term," she said. "They are Henry Ford and Edsel Ruddiman. I think I will put them together. Boys, you may take the last seat in the first row."

Henry and Edsel smiled shyly at each other. They were glad they were not in the front seat. They didn't know that Miss Nardin could see them just as well in the back seat as in the front seat. Her desk was on a raised platform at the front of the room. She had a clear view of all the pupils in the room.

Henry liked Edsel Ruddiman at once. Soon

they were the best of friends. Henry liked school, too, but he found it hard at times to keep his mind on his work.

One day several weeks after school had started, Henry was taking up more than his share of the seat. Edsel poked him in the ribs. "Move over, Henry," he whispered. "You're taking up all the room. I'll be on the floor the first thing you know."

Henry moved over. As usual, his pockets were bulging with a collection of screws and nuts and other things. It was when he reached into a pocket for something that he took up so much of the seat. He reached into a pocket now.

"What have you got?" Edsel whispered.

Henry glanced at Miss Nardin. She was writing a geography lesson on the blackboard for the boys and girls in the fifth grade. "What does it look like?" he whispered, holding something out in his hand.

"Oh, a jackknife," Edsel said. "Is it sharp?"

Henry didn't answer. Instead, he ran the blade across the edge of the desk. It left a smooth deep line in the wood. He carved another line beside the first one. Then he made four more to form the letters H and F.

Without a word he handed the knife to Edsel. Edsel carved his own initials, E A R, for Edsel Alexander Ruddiman.

Suddenly Miss Nardin's pointer came down across Edsel's fingers with a loud *whack*. Edsel jumped. *Whack!* The pointer came down on Henry's fingers, too, and Henry jumped. The boys had been so busy that neither of them had seen or heard her come up beside them.

"Stand up!" she ordered sternly.

Henry and Edsel rose slowly to their feet. They were too ashamed to look at her, so they stared down at their shoes.

"Now march to the blackboard, both of you,

and write this sentence: 'A fool's name is a fool's fame.' "

The other pupils started to giggle. The boys' faces turned red as they went to the blackboard.

"Return to your seats," Miss Nardin said when they had finished writing. "You will both stay in during recess. You will write that line about yourselves one hundred times. Is that clear?"

"Yes, ma'am," they said meekly.

Miss Nardin turned and went back to her desk.

"She must have eyes in the back of her head," Henry whispered to Edsel. "How did she know what we were doing?"

Recess wasn't much fun for the boys that day.

Henry Learns
to Farm

By the time spring came again Henry was old enough to help work in the fields. He learned to do many things on the farm that spring. He and John helped plant corn in the little holes Mike hoed ahead of them.

"Put six seeds to a hill," Mr. Ford told them. He taught them a little poem about planting corn, and Henry liked to say it each time he dropped seeds into a hole.

> One for the blackbird,
> One for the crow,
> One for the cutworm,
> And three to grow.

One hot day Margaret brought a pail of lemonade to the field. Everyone sat under a big oak tree and drank it. Henry was glad to have a chance to rest.

Mr. Ford wiped his forehead with a big red handkerchief. He looked across the field to the wood lot. The trees were so tall and so close together that sunlight could hardly find its way through the branches to the ground.

Henry watched a blackbird light on a scarred stump in the cornfield. It looked at him as if it were daring him to chase it away.

"He's looking for your corn, Henry."

"Why does—" Henry began, but Mr. Ford interrupted him.

"That's just the nature of birds," he said. "They like to have their meals shelled. Then they can go back to the trees and take a nap."

"We'll fix him," John put in. "We'll cut down all the trees."

Mr. Ford sighed. He remembered the work that had gone into clearing the land that was now being planted. It had been covered with huge oaks, elms, maples, and pines. He had cut

50

the branches of these trees into firewood and hauled the wood to Detroit to sell. He had hauled the big trunks to the sawmill, where they had been cut into lumber. Then he had piled the brush into huge stacks, usually with a stump in the middle, and set the stacks on fire.

The smaller stumps he had pulled out with horses, but the larger ones he had had to leave in the ground. When he had cleared the ground he had begun his planting. Only then had the land started to be a farm.

Now he pointed toward the wood lot. "Boys," he said, "we'll clear that next and then we'll have ten more acres for crops. One of these days we'll have enough land cleared for all of you to have farms of your own. Then you can plant your own crops and chase blackbirds out of your own fields."

Henry was silent for a moment. He couldn't imagine a farm big enough for all of them. Besides himself there were John and Margaret and Jane and baby William. That would mean a lot of land would have to be cleared.

"There must be an easier way to farm without all this hard work," he said.

His father looked at him sharply.

"Let me tell you something, Henry," he said. "There's nothing like land that you have cleared yourself. It's worth all the work that you have put into it just to get land that you can farm. Your own land is one thing that can't fly away."

Henry watched his father take up a handful of rich brown soil from the field and let it run through his fingers.

"No work is easy," Mr. Ford went on. "But it's much harder if you think it's hard."

Henry was not convinced. Farming seemed like a never-ending job and hard work to him. Men and horses had to do everything—all the plowing, planting, chopping, and hauling.

"There must be an easier way," he said again, stretching out under the tree. He folded his hands under his head and looked up at the sky. "Some day I'll think of a way to make farming easier. I know I will."

A TRIP IN THE WOODS

One afternoon a few weeks later Henry and John went for a walk with their father. They went to a swamp that lay along one side of Roulo Creek. Frogs were croaking so loudly they could be heard for a great distance.

"I'll bet there are a million, trillion frogs in that swamp," John said.

"Oh, John!" Henry scoffed. "There aren't that many frogs in the whole world."

"There are, too! We'll ask Father. He knows."

Whenever the boys wanted to know anything about birds or other animals they knew their

53

father could tell them. But even he didn't know how many frogs there were in the world.

"I can tell you how to tell a bullfrog from a green frog," he said. "I can even tell you how to predict the weather by the croak of the spring peeper. But I can't tell you how many frogs there are in this swamp."

"How can you predict weather by the croak of the spring peeper?" Henry demanded.

"Listen," his father replied. "That peeper is only an inch long but he croaks loudest of them all. He's telling us that it's going to be a warm day today."

"How do you know?" Henry asked.

"He's croaking fast. The faster he croaks the warmer the day will be. If it's going to be a cold day he slows up."

"Frogs look so funny sitting there blinking their big eyes and blowing up their stomachs," John laughed.

"I know a poem about that," Mr. Ford said.

"Of all the funny things that live
In woodland, marsh or bog,
That creep the ground or fly the air,
The funniest thing's the frog."

"Oh, I like that," Henry said. "I'll tell that to Margaret. She likes poems, especially the funny ones."

"Father," John said, "what became of all the tadpoles that used to be in the swamp?"

"You're looking at them, son. They've changed into frogs. First the mother frog lays eggs that hatch into tadpoles. After a while the tadpoles grow legs and lose their tails and then they become frogs."

A little farther on the boys saw a woodpecker on a maple tree. Mr. Ford taught them how to recognize the red-winged blackbird and the white-breasted nuthatch, and how to recognize

their songs. A bobolink called his own name from a tree when they passed by.

On the way back to the house Mr. Ford showed the boys a nest in the grass beside a log. He had plowed around the log so he would not disturb the four speckled eggs in it.

"It's a song sparrow's nest," he said. "Look up there." He pointed to a pine tree that stood alone at the edge of the field. "See the mother bird watching us up there? She doesn't have to carry on like that. We won't harm her eggs."

As they walked away the mother bird burst into song suddenly.

"Listen, Father," Henry said. "It sounds just as if she is singing *thank-e-e-e, thank-e-e-e*."

His father tousled his sandy curls. "Yes, son," he said. "She probably is singing *thank-e-e-e*. That little song sparrow likes it here on our farm. I can't say that I blame her. She picked one of the best farms in the state of Michigan.

"I think I know where there's something else that likes our farm," he added.

He led the boys to a corner of the field. There he stooped and parted the grass along the fence. All they could see was a hole in the ground.

"If we could see down in that hole we would find some baby rabbits," Mr. Ford said. "They'd all be blind—that is, they would be if they have just been born."

"Blind?" Henry gasped.

"Now don't worry about them. They'll see soon enough, but their eyes are closed when they're born. They'll be chewing at the corn before you know it. You know, Henry, I think you're old enough now to learn to handle a gun. How would you like that?"

"Oh, Father! Do you mean it?" Henry picked up a long stick, raised it to his shoulder and sighted down its length. "Bang! Bang! I got a rabbit!" Then he lowered the stick slowly and

58

looked at his father with a puzzled, worried expression. "You know, I don't know whether I want to kill anything or not," he said.

With a smile, Mr. Ford put his arm around Henry's shoulder and they started back to the barn. Soon he began to sing Henry's favorite song. Its quick rhythm made it a wonderful marching song. Henry and John fell into step beside him, and the three of them strode across the fields, singing at the tops of their voices.

> "Let the wealthy and great
> Roll in splendor and state;
> I envy them not, I declare it.
> I eat my own lamb,
> My own chickens and ham;
> I shear my own fleece and I wear it.
> I have lawns, I have bowers;
> I have fruits, I have flowers;
> The lark is my early alarmer.
> So, Jolly Boys, now
> Here's Godspeed the plough,
> Long life and success to the farmer."

Busy Days

"ANDY-OVER!" James shouted and threw a ball high over the schoolhouse roof.

"Andy-over!" Joe yelled from the other side, catching the ball. He threw it even higher than James did, and his team ran around the schoolhouse and caught the ball before James's side could get it.

The boys were playing Henry's favorite game during recess, but he was on his way to the well to fill the bucket with drinking water.

It was the first time Miss Nardin had asked Henry to get the water, and he was proud that she considered him big enough to carry the heavy wooden pail. Usually one of the older boys was given the job. But this was the spring term when the older boys were at home helping with the spring planting.

Henry thought if he hurried there would still be time to play Andy-over. He fastened the bucket on the rope fastened to the windlass and lowered it into the well. He flipped the rope so the bucket would tilt and not sink to the bottom. In a few minutes the bucket of water was pulling hard on the rope.

He started to crank the windlass, bringing the heavy bucket to the top of the well. The wet rope squeaked as it wound round the shaft, getting harder and harder to crank.

"If there was a machine to turn this thing, I wouldn't have to work so hard," Henry mumbled to himself.

The bucket was at the rim of the well when a ball hit him hard on the shoulder. He jumped so quickly the bucket began to teeter on the edge, but he held on to it and kept it from falling back into the well.

"Andy-over," James was shouting. "Henry, throw us the ball."

With one hand holding the bucket, Henry stretched the other, trying to reach the ball that had fallen a few feet away. He stretched so far that his hold on the bucket loosened and the crank started to spin. He quickly grabbed the handle and looked down into the well. The bucket was stopped halfway down.

"Henry, throw the ball!" several boys called.

Henry was puzzled. How could he throw the ball and hold the crank at the same time? Then he saw a piece of wood lying near his feet and he had the answer. He picked the wood up, wedged it between the handle and the shaft and slowly let go. The bucket remained where he had stopped it, halfway down the well.

The brake he had made left both of his hands free now. "Andy-over!" he called. He picked up the ball and threw it back toward the schoolhouse, as high as he could.

Turning back to the well, Henry was sorry that the older boys were not there to see his brake. They would all be back in school when the fall term started in September. He would have to wait until then to show them.

THE PUFFER WORKS

When Miss Nardin left the Scotch Settlement School she was followed by Mr. Ward. Henry liked Mr. Ward. He knew a lot about arithmetic, and Henry had discovered that he liked arithmetic better than any other subject that he studied.

After a year or so Mr. Ward moved to the Miller School. Henry got permission to go there,

too, so that Mr. Ward could continue to help him with arithmetic.

One day shortly after school had started, Henry and his friends were playing in the school yard during the lunch hour. Suddenly one of the boys came running into the schoolhouse.

"Mr. Ward! Mr. Ward! Come quick! Henry's set the fence on fire!"

Mr. Ward rushed outside with the water pail

and found Henry and his friends trying desperately to stop the fire. Dry grass was burning along the fence, and a post and some rails were blazing merrily. Mr. Ward threw the pail of water on the post and sent some boys for more. It took several pails of water to put the fire out, but at last there was nothing left but charred wood and grass.

"Henry!"

Henry stepped forward meekly. "Yes, sir."

"You will stay in after school today. Now all of you go back to the classroom."

Henry and the others went inside without a word. This was one noon hour they would not forget for a long time.

Henry should have worried about the punishment he was going to receive, but he didn't. All he could think of was the success of his "puffer," as the boys called it. It had worked! It had actually turned a wheel with steam.

Finally school was dismissed. When the room was empty, Mr. Ward looked up. "Come here, Henry," he said.

Henry went forward. He was a little worried now. He stood on one foot and then on the other. He looked down at his hands. He looked at the floor, at the ceiling, everywhere but at Mr. Ward's face.

"Now suppose you explain yourself, young man," said Mr. Ward severely.

"I made a puffer, sir. And the fire under the boiler spread and——"

"That much I know. But what is a puffer?"

"That's what the boys call it, sir. It's a kind of steam engine."

"What's this about a boiler? Do you mean you were using your mother's wash boiler?"

Henry looked at Mr. Ward. He wasn't smiling, but he wasn't angry, either. Was it possible he had never heard of a steam engine?

"Come, speak up, Henry."

"I had to have a boiler to make steam," he said. "I used an old oilcan."

"An oilcan!" Mr. Ward began to smile. "This is a tale if I ever heard one. Tell me more."

"Well, I made a hole in the oilcan for the steam to escape," Henry explained. "Then I soldered an upright arm on one side of the can and another on the other side. I made a hole in each arm and ran a shaft through the holes. Then I put a wheel on one end of the shaft and a four-bladed fan on the other end."

"That sounds like a fine piece of machinery, Henry," Mr. Ward interrupted, "but of what earthly good is it?"

"My goodness," Henry thought, "Mr. Ward may know a lot about reading and writing and arithmetic, but he doesn't know much about machinery. I'll have to draw him a picture."

He made a sketch of the puffer on his slate.

"We put water in the oilcan and put the oilcan in a pan," he said. "Then we made a fire under the pan. The fire made the water boil and turn to steam. The steam came out of the hole and turned the fan. The fan turned the shaft and made the wheel turn, too."

"Glory be!" Mr. Ward said under his breath. "The boy has figured out the principle of steam power. I can't be too hard on him. It would be a shame to discourage him."

"What did you say, Mr. Ward?"

"Never mind," Mr. Ward said sternly. "Tell me how the fence caught fire."

"I don't know, sir. I was too busy watching the steam to notice."

"Perhaps it will be punishment enough for you to tell your father that he will have to re-build the fence. On second thought, however, I want you to write this sentence one hundred times and bring it to me tomorrow."

68

He wrote on the blackboard, "When one means fails, try another."

"You'll find it in your *McGuffey Reader*," he said.

Henry nodded meekly and turned to go.

"When you were telling me about your engine just now you said, 'We did this' and 'We did that.' What did the other boys do?"

Henry grinned. "Oh, they filled the can with water and fetched the wood."

"That's what I thought," chuckled Mr. Ward. "I declare, Henry, some day you'll have everybody working for you!"

HENRY'S WORKBENCH

One evening a few days later, as Henry was bringing wood into the kitchen, he heard his mother talking.

"Anyway, I wish you would make one for

him," she was saying. "Maybe he'd do his experimenting here at home then. And just look at these trousers. These are the third pockets I've put in them already."

"All right, Mary," said Mr. Ford. "I'll make it tomorrow and have Henry help me. It is about time he learned that there is a place to do everything and a place to keep everything."

Henry stopped suddenly in the doorway. "Now that's a riddle," he thought. "Father is going to make something for me because I have holes in my pockets. What could it be?"

He tiptoed to the woodbox and laid the wood quietly in it. He didn't want his parents to know that he had overheard them.

"If they know I heard them maybe Father won't make whatever it is he's going to make."

Going back to the door, he opened it softly, then slammed it shut with a bang. Now they would know he was here.

"My, you're noisy," his mother said when he went into the sitting room. "Did you fill the woodbox, son?"

"Yes, Mama, the box is full," he said.

Mrs. Ford continued to sew and Mr. Ford continued to read his paper. Henry waited. He stood on one foot and then on the other. "Oh, I wish they would tell me," he thought.

Suddenly he said, "What are you going to do tomorrow, Father?"

"Work."

"What kind of work?"

"What kind of work does any farmer do?"

Henry sighed. There was no hope there. He would try his mother.

"Are those my trousers you're mending?"

"Do they look like John's?"

Henry sighed again. "I might as well give up," he thought. "They'll never tell me what they were talking about."

At that moment Mike entered the kitchen. "Henry, come here," he called. "I have something for you."

Henry hurried to the kitchen. Mike was standing with both hands behind his back.

"Which hand do you take?"

"The one with something in it," Henry smiled.

"Oh, no, you don't! Which hand?"

Henry chose the right hand. Mike opened it and Henry's eyes widened with pleasure and surprise. Mike's watch was in it!

"You mean you're going to give it to me?"

"Yes, it won't run any more, and what good is a watch if it won't tell you the time? I thought you might like to play with it."

"Thank you, Mike! Do I have to give it back if I make it run again?"

Mike chuckled. "If you can get that old thing to work again you can have it."

Clutching his new treasure, Henry ran back

to the sitting room, shouting, "Look! Look! See what Mike gave me!"

"That old watch isn't much good or Mike wouldn't have given it to you," his father said.

"That's all right. I'll make it run."

Henry pulled a chair close to the kerosene lamp and sitting on his heels laid the watch on the seat of the chair. Then he took out his jack-knife and started to pry off the back of the

watch. He had forgotten the strange conversation he had overheard.

Zing! A spring flew into the air and tiny cogs, screws, and other parts suddenly spilled over the seat of the chair.

Henry looked at them in dismay. Some of the parts were so little he could scarcely pick them up with his fingers. How could any of his father's screwdrivers fit into the heads of these little screws? How was he ever going to put the watch back together again? And he had been so sure he could make it run! "That's what I get for talking big," he thought unhappily.

"William, he simply must have a workbench," he heard his mother say. He looked up from the jumble of tiny parts.

A workbench! That was what they had been talking about. That was the answer to the riddle. His father was going to build him a workbench.

But Henry was still puzzled. "Mama, what do holes in my pockets have to do with a workbench?" he asked.

"Little pitchers have big ears, don't they?" she laughed. "See this nail?" She held up a flat-sided nail. "A workbench would be a much better place for it than your pocket."

Henry jumped up. "That's just what I need!" he cried. "That'll make a good screwdriver for these little screws."

"You can put the bench out in the dining room," his mother went on. "I don't want to find any more nails in your pockets. You'll have a place for everything and everything must be in its place."

Happily Henry slipped the nail into his pocket when his mother wasn't looking. What a wonderful day! He not only had a watch, but he was going to have a workbench, too.

The next morning he was up early to help his

father work on the bench. When it was finished, he stood back to look at it proudly. Then, glancing around to see whether his mother was watching, he took the nail from his pocket. He got a file and filed the nail until he had made a screwdriver just the right size for the heads of the screws in Mike's old watch.

"Now I need something to pick up these parts," he thought. "Something springy."

He thought for a moment, then went to his mother, who was washing dishes.

"Mama, do you have an old corset stay?"

"A corset stay? Sakes alive, Henry, what do you want with a corset stay?"

"I want to make some tweezers," he said. "Then I can pick up little wheels and screws without any trouble."

Mrs. Ford shook her head in wonder and went in search of a corset stay.

A Saturday
to Remember

HENRY HAD a problem. He and Edsel Ruddiman were going to Detroit with Mr. Ford and Grandpa O'Hern. Mr. Ford was going to deliver a load of wood to James Flower's machine shop. The problem was, how was Henry going to get inside that machine shop. He just had to get inside somehow.

Out in the yard the team was hitched to the wagon and eager to start. The horses shook their heads and jingled their harnesses as they waited impatiently for the last piece of wood to be loaded on the wagon.

"Here comes Edsel," John called.

77

Edsel broke into a trot and came breathlessly up the path. He was carrying a small package.

"You didn't have to bring your lunch, Edsel," Henry said. "Mama fixed us a picnic basket."

"This isn't my lunch," Edsel said, hiding the package behind his back.

"What is it, then?"

Edsel looked sheepish. "It's a package of herbs," he said.

Henry grinned. "I'm going to see Mr. Flower and I'll let him look at your flowers."

"They're not flowers," Edsel said angrily. "They're herbs."

"Flowers or herbs, they all look the same to me," Henry answered. "Mr. Flower should know whether they're flowers or not. That's his name, isn't it?"

"Mr. Flower isn't an apothecary," Edsel said furiously.

Henry laughed. "Don't get mad, Edsel. I was

only teasing. Where in the world did you learn that big word, anyway?"

"That's what I'm going to be when I grow up. I'm going to make medicine for people so they won't get sick. That's what an apothecary does. He makes medicines from herbs."

"I wondered why you were always picking those flowers," Henry said.

"Herbs!" Edsel shouted.

"Come on, boys," Grandpa called. "It's more than ten miles to Detroit and we want to get home before dark."

Henry and Edsel climbed up on the wagon and then still higher until they were perched on top of the wood.

"You look like a couple of Yankee Doodle Dandies up there," said Mr. Ford. "Giddap!"

"Yankee Doodle went to town," Henry started to sing.

Before long he slapped Edsel on the back.

"Listen, Edsel! I've made up some new words for Yankee Doodle. Listen!

> "Mr. Flower, he works all hours.
> We think it very funny.
> He doesn't know his name will cure
> A sore and aching tummy."

They sang it over and over and soon Grandpa and Mr. Ford joined in. Before long they were all tired of the song.

"Edsel," Henry whispered, "you must help me get inside the machine shop."

"How can I help? Can't you just walk in?"

"Don't be silly. You know Father will want to leave as soon as we unload the wood. Can't you get sick or something? Then you'd have to be carried inside the shop and I could help to take you in."

"Henry Ford, are you crazy! I can't do a thing like that and you know it."

80

"I know," Henry admitted grudgingly. "I guess I'll have to think of something else."

"I don't want to see a smelly old machine shop anyhow," Edsel said. "I want to go to Stearns's Apothecary Shop."

"So that's why you brought those flow— herbs," Henry smiled.

The "corduroy" road was made of thick logs laid side by side. It was so rough the boys were bounced from one side of the wagon to the other. Finally they jumped down and walked and ran beside the horses.

Before long they were on the Michigan Avenue plank road. The horses' slow plodding increased to a fast walk, and the planks rattled under the wagon.

"You'd better ride, now," Mr. Ford called to the boys. "There are some warped planks ahead and you might stub your toes on them."

There were not only warped planks but rotten

81

ones, too. In some places the road dipped crazily to one side. Three times Mr. Ford had to stop to let another wagon by or his own would have toppled off the road.

The trip didn't seem very long to the boys. The first thing they knew, they had reached the tollgate five miles from the center of town.

"Here's a nickel to pay the toll, Henry," his father said. "It's a penny a mile, so you won't get any change. Mind you, don't drop it."

Grandpa's eyes twinkled. "No, for goodness' sake don't drop it. They need that nickel to fix this road."

Soon the boys could see the church spires of the city, then smoke from the smokestacks of factories down by the river. At last they reached the heart of the city. Here there were buildings six stories high. The horses' hoofs made a different sound because the streets were paved with cedar blocks.

82

There was so much to see that Henry and Edsel sat wide-eyed. Henry almost forgot about the machine shop and Edsel the apothecary shop. They saw fancy carriages everywhere. They saw delivery wagons and big drays loaded with heavy boxes and barrels. Here and there one of the new high-wheeled bicycles darted in and out between the carriages and wagons. Along the wooden sidewalks women held their skirts up to keep them out of the dust.

Woodward Avenue stretched ahead in a long straight line, with shops on either side. It finally ended at the Detroit River. The boys could see a ferryboat tied up at the wharf, puffing smoke, while it loaded passengers who were going across the river to Canada.

Mr. Ford turned off Woodward Avenue onto a dirt street. At last he drew up behind the Flower Machine Shop. By this time Henry's heart was pounding with excitement.

"Come on, boys, give us a hand with this wood," Mr. Ford called.

Henry wasn't much help. He couldn't keep his eyes away from the door of the shop. At last Mr. Flower came out.

"Hello there, Will," he said. "How are you, Mr. O'Hern?" The three men stood talking together near the door.

Henry slipped over to where they were standing. He had his watch in his hand.

"Hello there, Henry," Mr. Flower said. "And the Ruddiman boy, Edsel, isn't it?" He smiled. "Have you made any more puffers, Henry?"

Henry blushed. "No, but I fixed this watch, Mr. Flower. Mike gave it to me."

Mr. Flower studied the watch and then Henry's eager face. He turned to Mr. Ford.

"When are you going to let this young fellow come to work for me, Will? He's a natural-born mechanic if I ever saw one."

"Don't hold your breath till that happens, Jim," Mr. Ford said. "Henry's a farmer. Anyway, don't you think he's a little young?"

Henry didn't hear the rest of the conversation. He had slipped away and was standing by the door, peering inside. The magic world of belts, pulleys and the smell of hot oil and metal was within his reach.

Mr. Ford had to call twice before Henry heard him. "Henry! Come on, we have to go."

Reluctantly Henry turned away and climbed in the empty wagon. "Where are we going, Father?" he asked without enthusiasm.

His father's answer surprised him. "You and Edsel are pretty big boys now. How would you like to stay in town while Grandpa and I go to see your Aunt Rebecca?"

Henry's heart thumped and he squeezed Edsel's arm with excitement. He couldn't believe his ears. But he mustn't seem too eager.

"We'll be all right, Father," he said. "You don't have to worry about us."

"We'll take the horses to Wade's blacksmith shop. They each need a couple of new shoes. Now don't go off Woodward Avenue, and we'll meet you at the blacksmith's in two hours."

Grandpa handed each of the boys a penny. "You can buy yourself a peppermint stick." A twinkle came in his eye. "Don't spend all your money in one place," he laughed.

Clang! Clang! A bell warned them that a horsecar was coming. Mr. Ford and Grandpa climbed aboard. They waved to the boys as the car started down the street.

Henry and Edsel went back to the blacksmith shop. They watched the bellows for a while, but somehow they weren't really interested in them today. Besides, Mr. Wade wouldn't answer Henry's questions.

"Let's spend our pennies," Edsel said. Usually

87

peppermint candy would have occupied them for some time. Today, however, neither of the boys was interested in candy. They broke the sticks in two and put the pieces in their pockets to be enjoyed later.

Then they stood in front of the candy shop, looking up and down Woodward Avenue. The street didn't look half so exciting as it had when they first saw it. Something else was drawing them like a magnet.

Henry looked at Edsel. Edsel looked at Henry. Suddenly they grinned at each other.

"I'll see you later, Henry," Edsel said.

They parted, each going his own way.

LOST—TWO BOYS

When Mr. Ford and Grandpa O'Hern returned to the blacksmith shop two hours later, Henry and Edsel were gone. Mr. Ford asked the blacksmith, Mr. Wade, what had become of them.

"I don't know, Will," Mr. Wade said. "I was glad when they left. That boy of yours asked so many questions I had to shoo him out."

"We'll go to the candy shop first," Mr. Ford decided. "Henry likes candy."

"Yes, the boys were here," the clerk said. "But they didn't say where they were going."

A crowd was gathering at the watering trough, but the boys were not in the crowd.

"You don't suppose they went down to the river?" Mr. Ford said anxiously. The two men trudged in and out of shops along Woodward Avenue, searching. They asked strangers and one or two neighbors whether they had seen the boys. But no one had.

"I guess we'd better go down to the river," Mr. Ford said at last.

"Wait a minute, Will," Grandpa exclaimed

suddenly. "We're certainly not using good sense. I'll bet I can find Henry."

"Where?"

"In Jim Flower's machine shop, of course!"

"He wouldn't go back there. I told him not to go off Woodward Avenue."

Grandpa O'Hern looked hard at Mr. Ford. "Will," he said, "I reckon you just don't want to admit that Henry is more interested in machines than he is in minding his Pa."

Mr. Ford scowled, but he had to admit that Grandpa might be right.

When they reached the machine shop they found Henry watching Jim Flower as he took a piece of copper pipe from a machine. Henry's eyes were as bright as the copper itself. He watched the machinist closely as he took the pipe to another machine close by.

"Here, Henry," Mr. Flower said, "take this home and see what you can make with it." He handed Henry a little piece of the copper pipe that he had cut on the machine.

Henry was so busy watching that he didn't see his father enter the shop. He didn't hear him call until Mr. Ford shouted in his ear. But the moment he saw his face Henry knew that his father was angry. For a second he was frightened. But the magic world of machines that had opened up for him today made even the thought of punishment seem unimportant.

He clutched the piece of copper pipe in his hand and meekly followed his father and grandfather up the street. He was still thinking about the machines he had seen.

"Henry," his father said sternly, "I'm asking you a question! Where's Edsel?"

"Oh! Oh, he's over at Stearns's Apothecary Shop, I suppose."

"No wonder we couldn't find him. That's on Woodbridge near the river. Fred Stearns isn't likely to want a young scamp like Edsel getting in his way."

They found Edsel right where Henry said he would be. But Frederick Stearns wasn't a bit annoyed with the "young scamp." With their heads together, he and Edsel were examining the package of herbs that Edsel had brought to town.

"We've come to keep this young scamp from bothering you," said Mr. Ford.

Mr. Stearns laughed. "Bothering me? Nothing of the kind. This boy knows more about herbs than anyone around here. We've just made a business deal. I'm going to buy my herbs from him."

"Well, I swan!" said Grandpa. "You boys have had quite a day."

"Now don't forget, Edsel," Mr. Stearns called as they started for the door. "I can use fennel, senna, and tansy."

Edsel nodded, then he, too, meekly walked toward the blacksmith shop.

Two tired but excited boys huddled on the floor of the empty wagon on the way home. By the time they had reached the Fords' barnyard darkness had come. Even so, Henry and Edsel had not had enough time to tell each other everything that had happened to them that day.

A Good-Luck Piece

SPRING HAD come again, and the smaller children were playing in the yard. Henry could hear them through the open window above his workbench. They were laughing and shouting. It was a beautiful day, but Henry didn't feel like playing. He didn't feel like laughing or shouting. His mother had died that winter, and the house seemed quiet and empty without her.

Henry stared at the neat rows of tools on his workbench. After his visit to the Flower Machine Shop last summer he had rearranged the tools completely. He had tried to make the bench look like the ones he had seen there.

But he hadn't used it much this spring. The parts of two watches that he had promised to fix for neighbors still lay in the boxes he kept them in. In one corner of the bench lay the piece of copper pipe that Jim Flower had given him that day.

Henry picked up the pipe and studied it. It was just a piece of copper pipe, but it had been made into a cylinder in a real machine shop. For that reason it was different.

As he was looking at the pipe, his cousin Jane Flaherty touched him on the shoulder. Jane was keeping house for the Fords now that Mrs. Ford had died.

"Henry," she said, "if you can tear yourself away from that workbench, there's something I'd like you to do."

"I'm busy," Henry said without looking up.

Jane leaned down and whispered in his ear. "It's Margaret," she said. "I'm worried about her.

You know, she misses her mother terribly. Won't you see if you can cheer her up?"

Henry nodded and went to find Margaret.

"You're the only one who can do it," Jane called after him.

"It shouldn't be hard to make Margaret laugh," Henry thought. "She's always laughing." But he would do as Jane asked, then go back to his work. He wanted to do something with that piece of copper pipe.

Henry found Margaret on the back steps with the other children. Jane was feeding baby Robert lumps of brown sugar, getting more on his face than in his mouth. William was trying, without much success, to button his shoes. Margaret was sitting at one side, crying silently.

Henry looked at her in bewilderment. "What shall I do?" he wondered. But he had promised Cousin Jane that he would try to make Margaret laugh, so he had to do something.

While he was wondering what to do, William came clumping across the porch. His toes were turned in and he teetered from side to side to keep from stumbling. He looked very comical.

Henry laughed loudly. "Look at William!" he cried. "Look, Margaret, he's pigeon-toed!"

Jane and William started to laugh, and even Robert gurgled through his sugar. But Margaret stared into space without a trace of a smile.

Henry looked at her in despair. "If that won't make her laugh I don't know what will," he thought. "What shall I do?"

Suddenly William stumbled over his own feet and fell headfirst into Margaret's lap. It made her angry. She shook him until he started to howl. Cousin Jane came running from the kitchen, and little Jane raced around the porch yelling for no reason at all.

"William!" Margaret shook him angrily. "You have your shoes on the wrong feet!"

"How can he have them on the wrong feet?"
Henry shouted above the uproar. "Those are
the only feet he has! Isn't that funny, Margaret?
Those are the only feet he has. Don't you get the
joke? Those are the only——"

Margaret glared at him and ran sobbing into
the house.

"Henry, what in the world did you do to her?" Cousin Jane asked sharply.

"Nothing," Henry said in bewilderment. "I just tried to cheer her up, that's all."

"And a fine job you did!"

"Girls!" Henry snorted disgustedly. "I give up!" And with that he stomped back to his workbench in the dining room.

In no time at all, as he worked there, he forgot the excitement Cousin Jane thought he had caused. He was making something with the piece of pipe.

He couldn't use good metal like this for just anything. He had to make something special, and his work had to be just right. First he drilled a tiny hole near one end of the pipe. Then, working slowly and carefully, he closed the end of the pipe with solder.

It was suppertime before he had finished. The teakettle was singing on the kitchen stove. Margaret, with a gloomy expression on her face, was stirring a pot of stew.

Henry slipped up behind her and moved the teakettle to the hottest part of the stove. He put the pipe over the spout of the kettle, then stepped back and waited.

Suddenly the kettle began to whistle shrilly. Margaret jumped and screamed, and Henry burst into laughter. Margaret stared at the kettle. Henry had made a whistle out of the pipe, and the steam was making it blow.

Margaret started to laugh herself. "Henry Ford, you almost scared the living daylights out of me," she cried. She swung at him with her spoon. Henry ducked and ran into the dining room, with Margaret close behind.

Cousin Jane stood with her mouth wide open. "What in the world are you two doing?"

"I scared her," Henry laughed. He dodged behind Jane and held her between Margaret

100

and himself. "I put a whistle on the kettle and it scared her when the steam made it blow."

"It's a lucky thing for us you made a whistle out of that precious piece of pipe," Jane said. "We'd better call it your good-luck piece."

And that's just what it was—Henry's good-luck piece.

A New Kind of Teakettle Lid

ONE DAY Henry and his father went to Detroit. As they jogged along Henry listened idly to his father's words and watched the countryside as they passed slowly through it. Suddenly a strange noise brought him to with a start. It was made up of hisses, rattles, and clanks, the like of which he had never heard before.

He looked ahead, and his eyes popped wide open with astonishment.

"Father! Look! A steam road engine!"

Sure enough, a steam engine was coming up the road, wheezing and clanking and rattling, at a slow but steady pace. Smoke spurted from its

smokestack and dust rose in thick clouds from behind its wheels.

It was the first steam road engine Henry had seen. Without another word he jumped down from the wagon and ran forward as fast as his legs would carry him. When he reached the engine he recognized its driver.

"Mr. Reden! Hello, Mr. Reden!" he called. "May I ride with you?" Fred Reden worked for one of the Fords' neighbors, Mr. Gleason.

"What's that, Henry?" Mr. Reden answered, cupping his hand to his ear.

"May I ride on the engine?" Henry yelled.

"Can't hear you."

"I'd like a ride!" By this time Henry was out of breath. "P-please, Mr. Reden, may I climb on?" he shouted at the top of his voice.

"This danged thing makes more noise than a locomotive crossing a loose bridge. Can't hear a thing you're saying, Henry."

Henry gave up. He stopped where he was and sadly watched the engine roll down the road. It had gone several yards before he heard Mr. Reden laugh.

"Come on, Henry. I was only joking. I knew what you wanted. You'll have to be quick, though. I can't stop this thing by saying, 'Whoa.' It isn't like a horse."

Henry dashed forward and climbed on board. "Where are you going?" he wanted to know.

"Right now I'm going to Mr. Gleason's farm," Fred Reden said. "But I'll tell you something. There's a farmer down the road, name of William Ford. Has a pretty good farm, too. He's going to be threshing soon, and I think he may try out this engine. Do you know him?"

"Does he have a boy named Henry who likes engines?" Henry asked with a serious expression. He knew Mr. Reden was teasing him, but he didn't let on.

"Yes, that's the one. His Pa tells me he's not much for farming, but he can fix about anything around the place that needs fixing."

"I guess that's about right," Henry laughed.

"Put more coal in the firebox, Henry. We need to have steam to make this engine run."

Henry opened the firebox door and threw in a few pieces of coal. The steam seemed to hiss a little more loudly.

"How many revolutions do the wheels make a minute?" he asked importantly.

"Ha! Where did you learn that big word?"

Henry blushed. "I heard the men at Flower's Machine Shop in Detroit talking about revolutions. I know what the word means, too."

"Now don't get your dander up," Fred Reden laughed. "I was just surprised you knew such a big word."

"I like engines, Mr. Reden," Henry said. "I want to learn more about them."

"All right, then. Do you know who James Watt was?"

Henry shook his head.

"Well, he was a Scotch inventor. He died about fifty years before you were born. He was the man who captured steam, you might say, and put it to work."

"I tried to capture steam in a teakettle once. Mama said I'd burn myself."

"Probably you would. The lid jumped up and down, didn't it? Well, sir, that steam was jumping up and down yelling, 'Let me out! Let me out! I'm too big for this kettle.' That's what happens to steam. It expands or spreads out. You can't let it go just anywhere, though. You have to capture it."

"Then when you capture it, you put it to work," Henry said.

"That's the idea. James Watt noticed that steam would lift a teakettle lid, too. That made him think that steam might lift other things as well as a lid. So he made a machine in which steam moved a kind of lid called a piston. This piston made a wheel go round."

"I know!" Henry exclaimed. "The pressure of the steam pushed the piston back and forth."

Mr. Reden looked at Henry in surprise. "It sure beats me how a young farm boy like you can understand machinery so well. I guess your Pa would be a lot happier if you were just as smart about farming."

Henry didn't hear him. He was lost in thought. "If a steam engine can pull this road engine, why can't it pull anything on four wheels?" he asked himself.

"Here comes your Pa," Fred Reden went on. "He'd better pull over to the side of the road or that team will run away. Horses aren't used to steam engines yet."

Mr. Ford did stop his team. The horses reared

on their hind legs as the engine approached. Mr. Ford pulled hard on the reins. "Whoa, there! Whoa there, boys!" He had a hard time calming them down.

"Hello, Father," Henry called, jumping to the ground.

"I thought you'd be riding on that thing," Mr. Ford said. "I'm surprised you weren't running it. Has he told you how it works yet, Fred?"

"He knows," said Mr. Reden with a laugh.

Mr. Ford laughed, too. "I thought so. Anything about machines and engines Henry knows. I wish he knew as much about farming."

Mr. Reden looked at Henry slyly. "Guess your Pa understands you, Henry," he said.

Henry lowered his eyes. "I guess he does," he said with a shamefaced grin.

A Bargain
with John

LITTLE PUDDLES of water stood in the path, but Henry didn't bother to step around them. He liked the squishy sound his boots made as he splashed through the water. Anyway, he was in a hurry. He was on his way to Roulo Creek to see whether his paddle wheel was still there.

The winter Henry was fourteen had been the worst that anyone in Michigan could remember. One snowstorm had followed another. Blizzards drifted the snow higher than Henry's head, and everything had been covered with snow and ice. The creeks and streams that flowed into the Rouge River had frozen solid.

110

Now the woods were bursting with spring. As Henry hurried along he saw a clump of fennel growing beside the path. Edsel would like to know about that.

When he reached the creek he found a tree, split by frost, stretching from one side of the creek to the other. It was in the very spot where he had put his paddle wheel. There wasn't a sign of the wheel.

"That wheel is probably in the Detroit River by now," he thought. He was sorry. It had been a good paddle wheel. He and the rest of the boys had had fun playing with it.

He sat on a fallen tree. A frog croaked and jumped into the creek. "Don't croak at me, Mr. Frog," Henry laughed. "Of all the funny things that live, the funniest thing's the frog." It had been a long time since his father had taught him that silly verse. That was the day he had first been allowed to help plant corn. "One for the blackbird, one for the crow."

Crows were having trouble finding corn now. His father had bought a new corn planter. It covered the corn with earth as soon as it touched the ground.

"If I could pull that corn planter with some kind of power instead of horses, I wouldn't mind being a farmer," Henry thought.

Ever since Mr. Flower had told his father

that Henry was a natural-born mechanic, Henry had been thinking about machines and reading everything he could find about them. The farm chores were growing more and more unpleasant.

"It isn't that I don't like living on a farm," he thought. "I do like it. And I know Father wants me to be a farmer. He's always talking about buying more land so that each of us can have a farm. But—" he threw a clump of dirt into the creek—"why can't I be satisfied? Why don't I like to farm as much as John does, I wonder?"

"Henry! Where are you?"

Henry sighed. John had found him at last.

"Can't a fellow get away by himself once in a while?" he asked, a little annoyed. "I came down to see whether the paddle wheel was still here or not."

"Oh, it's gone!" John cried. "Will you make another one, Henry?"

"No, that's for children," Henry said.

113

"That's mean, Henry. I liked it."

"Well, if I did make one I'd put a grinder on the shaft. Then we could use it to grind things."

"Please make another one, Henry," John said. "I'll help you."

Henry didn't answer. He threw a branch into the stream and watched it whirl and twist in the current. "Hurry up," he said to the branch. "Maybe you'll catch up with the paddles in the Detroit River."

John chuckled. "Maybe they didn't get that far. I'll bet they're stuck in the bank by the railroad bridge."

Henry almost fell over backward. "The railroad bridge! How could I have forgotten that!" He jumped to his feet. "John, I'll make you another paddle wheel, a big one. But you'll have to pay me for it."

John stared at him. "Pay you for it? Are you crazy? How can I——"

114

Henry interrupted him. "Tomorrow they're putting a new railroad bridge across the river."

"I know that! Everyone will be there. Father said we could go, too."

"Listen, John," Henry said. "You know the men will start to work early in the morning. I want to be there as soon as they begin."

"You mean you want me to do your work so you can get there early?"

"Please, John, will you? I'll make you a wonderful paddle wheel."

John agreed, and the bargain was made.

A COWCATCHER RIDE

The next morning Henry was half a mile from home before the roosters started to crow. He took a shortcut through the woods.

He reached the riverbank where the new bridge was to be built. He peered through the

115

bushes into the clearing. He could hear men talking, but there was no one in sight.

Smoke poured from a locomotive standing on the tracks. Behind it was a derrick, with its boom raised and its chains dangling in the air. Near by were heaps of rails, long beams for the bridge and railroad ties.

Henry crept from his hiding place and made a beeline for the locomotive.

"Hey there, young feller! Where d'you think you're going?" A workman appeared from nowhere and seized him by the elbow.

"I—I was just going to look at the engine," Henry stammered.

"You were, were you? Well, you can just look at it from over yonder. We can't have young boys hanging around here when we have work to do. Now get out of here!"

"But—but I know all about steam engines, Mister. I can help you," Henry said eagerly.

116

The man roared with laughter. "Listen to that now! Hey, Pat!" he yelled. "You'd better get over here. There's a young feller here who thinks he can do your job!"

The workmen laughed, and Henry retreated to the riverbank with a red face. "Maybe I didn't make such a good bargain with John after all," he thought.

Soon the men began on the new bridge and Henry forgot his disappointment. The locomotive went back and forth across the bridge. Workmen jumped on and off, replacing rotting beams and ties with new ones. Above the noise and confusion, Henry could hear the foreman shouting, "Hurry up! Get a move on, men! We'll have to let that passenger train through at noon."

As the sun rose higher a crowd began to gather. People stood in groups, watching and talking. There were so many people that Henry had a chance to slip closer to the engine.

"Hi, Henry!" Edsel and James Ruddiman and several other boys came running forward.

"Hello," said Henry halfheartedly.

"Let's play leapfrog," someone suggested.

"Who wants to play leapfrog today?" Henry asked scornfully.

Before anyone could answer, a cheer rose from the crowd. "Here she comes! Clear the tracks! Here comes the train!"

Henry slipped quickly through the crowd and was the first to reach the train as it slowed for the bridge. As the train started across, the crowd cheered again. But Henry wasn't in the crowd. He was sitting on the engine's cowcatcher with his feet stuck out in front of him, waving to the people on the bank.

Pat scratched his head. "Well, I'll be doggoned if it isn't that young scamp who wanted my job!"

An Important Decision

"HERE ARE your lunch pails," Margaret said. "Hurry now, or you'll be late to school."

Henry sat at the kitchen table but made no move to leave with the other children. He watched Margaret clear the table and busy herself about the kitchen. She was keeping house for the family now, and the responsibility rested heavily on her twelve-year-old shoulders. It seemed only yesterday to Henry that he had frightened her with his steam whistle and she had chased him with a spoon. But here she was, doing a woman's work.

Henry looked out the window. It was fall.

Bare trees and brown fields were as dull as the cloudy sky, but cold weather had not come yet.

"The crops are in," Henry was thinking. "And now that winter has come, work won't be so heavy here on the farm. John can do a lot of it, and William can help with the lighter chores. It isn't as if I were leaving Father alone."

"Henry Ford! Are you still here?" Margaret abruptly interrupted his thoughts. "You're going to be late for school." She shoved a lunch pail into his hands and gave him a gentle push toward the door.

He got as far as the road, then turned and hurried back to the kitchen.

"Good-by Margaret," he called cheerfully.

Margaret looked surprised. "Well, good-by yourself. You'd think you were going a million miles away instead of two miles."

When Henry reached the short cut through the woods toward the school he did not take it.

Instead he hurried down the corduroy road leading to Detroit. He had made an important decision that morning. He was leaving the farm and was going to work in Detroit. Now that he was sixteen, he thought he was old enough to think and act for himself.

He didn't know why he had to go this very day. He just felt that he had to keep on walking until he reached the city and Jim Flower's machine shop. He was sorry about leaving without saying good-by to his father. But he remembered that his father had once said, "A man must do what he has to do."

"In the shop I'll have a set of real tools to work with, not nails and knitting needles," Henry told himself. "I'll learn how to run all kinds of machines and how to make all kinds of parts."

The magic world of lathes, grinders, shafts and pulleys lay just ahead of him.

Suddenly his daydreaming was interrupted by

a fearful thought. "What if Mr. Flower can't use another apprentice?"

He put this thought out of his mind. Mr. Flower had said he was a natural-born mechanic, and where did a natural-born mechanic belong but in a machine shop? Besides, didn't he have his good-luck piece with him?

By this time he had reached a stretch of gravel road where the plank road had once been. As he walked along, he was startled by the sound of a trotting horse. He looked up just as a young man in a stylish buggy drew up beside him.

"Hello, there," the young man said with a friendly smile. "Do you want a ride?"

Gratefully Henry climbed into the buggy. A ride would get him to Detroit that much sooner. The young man was a stranger, and Henry was glad of that. A neighbor would have wanted to know why Henry was going to town alone.

"How far are you going?" the man asked.

"Detroit," Henry answered confidently. "I'm going to work in the Flower Machine Shop."

"I'm a traveling salesman myself," the young man said. "I wouldn't know where there's a machine shop, but I'll let you off at Metcalf's Dry Goods Store."

"That'll be fine," Henry said.

The miles passed quickly. The salesman kept up a steady conversation. He didn't seem to expect Henry to answer him, only to listen. Henry listened, but not very closely. He had other things to think about.

They passed the tollgate on Michigan Avenue. "You say you're going to work in a machine shop," the salesman said as the horse trotted toward the city. "Where do you live?"

Without thinking, Henry started to say, "On a farm in Dearborn Township." Then he thought, "What a fool I am! I hadn't even thought about that." But in the next moment he had an answer. "I live with my aunt."

At last the salesman reached Metcalf's Dry Goods Store. "This is as far as I go," he said.

Henry thanked him and started off toward the machine shop.

Getting a job with Mr. Flower was much easier than Henry had ever dreamed or hoped. It was so simple that he had to laugh when he remembered how worried he had been.

Mr. Flower looked up when Henry entered

the shop. "Well, Henry," he said, "you can start by helping Tom over there."

"How—how did you know what I wanted?" Henry stammered.

"You brought your lunch pail, didn't you?"

Then and there Henry started his apprenticeship. His workbench was his school desk and the men in the shop were his teachers. He learned how to use many kinds of machines. He learned also to make parts for engines and helped to install them.

Henry liked working at the Flower shop. However, as an apprentice, he did not earn enough to pay for his room and board. Somehow, somewhere, he had to earn more money.

One evening on his way home he noticed a number of watches and clocks in the window of a jewelry store. He entered and asked the owner, Mr. McGill, if he needed someone to clean and repair watches.

"I could use someone," Mr. McGill said, "but a young fellow like you wouldn't know how to repair watches."

"I can fix watches," Henry said confidently. "Let me show you."

He got the job and worked at night after he had worked all day in the machine shop.

"You'll have to work in the back room," Mr. McGill told him. "I don't want my customers

126

to see a young sprout like you working on their watches. They'd never come back."

After about a year Henry left the Flower shop and went to work in another shop, where he could learn more about steam engines. At last, after three years, he finished his apprenticeship. Now he was a full-fledged machinist.

But three years spent with machines and steam engines had given Henry ideas that he wanted to try out. One day he met Jim Flower on the street.

"Well, Henry," Mr. Flower said, "you're a real machinist now—in fact, about the best machinist that ever came out of our shop. What are you going to do now?"

Henry thought for a moment. "I think I'll go home," he answered. "I want to learn more about steam engines and I need time to study them and think. I want to try out some ideas, too. So I think I'll go back to the farm."

Time to Think and Plan

HENRY WENT home to the farm that he didn't like. However, he didn't farm much, except to help his father. He spent many hours working in the shop that he had made in the tool shed. When summer came he ran the steam engine for Mr. Gleason's threshing machine. Then he went to work for the Westinghouse Air-Brake Company. This company made steam engines. Henry's job was to see that all their engines in southern Michigan were in good order.

His job took him away from home a good part of the time, but he liked that. He liked meeting new people and seeing new places. Above all, he liked to find new problems involving engines. Each time he came home he would hurry to his shop to try some new experiment that his work had suggested.

One time he was called to Detroit to repair an engine at the Eagle Iron Works. When he arrived, he discovered that the engine was a gas engine. He had never seen one before.

As he worked on the engine he began to think about something that had been taking shape in his mind for some time. It was an idea that he had had ever since he saw Fred Reden driving a steam engine down the road.

He wanted to make some kind of machine that would lighten the farmer's work and make it easier to haul things from one place to another. Much of his thought and time lately had been given to such a machine.

"Henry," his father said one night, "are you going to be home tomorrow?"

They were sitting in the dining room after supper. Mr. Ford was reading a newspaper and Henry was looking at a magazine, while Margaret did the dishes.

"Yes, I think so," Henry said. "Why?"

"I need help pulling the stumps in that new field we cleared last winter."

"I'll get them for you, Father," Henry said. "You needn't bother."

He was up and out of the house the next morning before anyone else was awake. It was a beautiful fall day. When the sun came up it shone in a clear sky, and there was a pleasant tang in the air.

As the rest of the family were eating breakfast they heard a clanging, hissing noise outdoors. William looked out the window.

"It's Henry!" he exclaimed. "He has Mr. Gleason's steam engine."

Mr. Ford rushed to the door and called out,

"What are you planning to do with that fool contraption?"

"Come to the new field and see," Henry called as he clanked away.

When Mr. Ford drove his team of strong horses to the field later he found Henry at work.

"How can you pull stumps with that clumsy thing?" Mr. Ford demanded. "Let me get them. These horses can do a better job."

Henry just smiled. He had learned a long time ago not to argue with his father. But he was determined to prove how much better an engine could do the work than horses.

He had fastened a heavy chain to the rear of the engine. Now he climbed down and fastened the loose end of the chain around a large stump. Then he climbed back on the engine and started it forward. It puffed and grunted. Suddenly the stump came out with a muffled sound.

Henry looked slyly at his father, who was trying to quiet the horses. Mr. Ford stared at the engine briefly with dislike. Then without a word he turned the horses and went back to the house.

Henry smiled again but almost at once grew serious. "Father's right," he thought. "This engine is a clumsy contraption. It's too big and slow, and too hard to operate. Surely there's some kind of engine in the world that can do a better job than this." He thought of the gas engine he had repaired in Detroit.

At this point his thoughts were interrupted by voices. He turned and saw Margaret and Jane and a third girl whom he had met a few nights before. Each of the girls had a basket.

Henry got down from the engine and went toward the girls.

"Henry, you remember Clara Bryant from Greenfield, don't you?" Margaret said.

Henry nodded and smiled bashfully.

Jane pulled at his sleeve. "Come on, Henry,

help us shake a hickory tree. There aren't enough nuts on the ground to fill our baskets."

"I'll show you an easy way to get nuts," Henry said. "Come on, get on the engine."

The girls didn't need a second invitation. They scrambled up. Henry put Clara on the seat beside him, while Margaret and Jane hung on as best they could.

Henry drove in and out between the stumps until he reached the edge of the woods, where there were several hickory trees.

"This tree has the most nuts," he said. "Hang on tight and cover your heads!"

He drove the engine against the tree, giving it a strong push. The tree shook and nuts fell to the ground like hailstones.

The girls squealed with delight. Clara looked at Henry in amazement. "Why, he's the smartest boy I've ever met!" she thought.

And Henry, as he helped her down from the

engine, thought, "She's the prettiest girl I've ever met!"

Henry helped the girls fill their baskets. Then he returned to pulling stumps.

That night after supper he began to think about engines again. His father was right. Steam engines were too big and clumsy to use in a workable road machine. He would have to learn more about gasoline engines.

He sat staring at the floor for a moment. "Clara has brown eyes," he thought suddenly, and forgot all about engines.

THE FOUR-HANDED WATCH

"Henry," Margaret said one evening at supper, "there's a dance at Martindale Hall over in Greenfield Township. Would you like to go?"

"Yes," Henry said. "I like square dances."

Soon he and John and Margaret and Jane

were bundled up and on the way. The sleigh glided silently over the snow-packed road. When they reached the hall, it took Henry a while to find a place to hitch the horse and cover him with a blanket. Then he went inside, where the dance had already started.

He stood in the doorway for a moment, stamping the snow from his shoes and looking around.

"Hello, Henry," someone said.

Henry turned and saw Clara Bryant standing beside him. His face turned red with embarrassment. "Hello, Clara," he muttered.

"Well, Henry," Clara said, "what time did you get here?"

With a flourish Henry took his watch from his pocket and studied it carefully. "It depends on how you look at it," he said.

"What do you mean?" Clara demanded. "I just asked you a simple question."

Henry caught her arm as she turned away.

"Look!" he said. "Look at my watch!"

Clara looked at it. It had two dials, one within the other, and two pairs of hands, one red and the other black.

"But, Henry, why do you need two sets of hands on a watch?"

"Well, do you remember how puzzled everyone was last summer when the new standard time zones were started?"

"Yes, nobody could keep the old sun time and the new standard time straight."

"Well, I made a watch that tells time for both. See, the black hands tell sun time, and the red hands tell standard time."

Clara was impressed. "Henry, how clever!" The rest of the evening time meant little to either of them, whether it was standard time or sun time. They were having too much fun. And when the evening was over Clara was sure that Henry was the smartest boy in the county. As for Henry, he was sure that Clara was the smartest and prettiest girl in the world.

One day a few months later Henry and his father were working together in the barn. "Henry," Mr. Ford said, "you know that Moir farm I bought a long time ago?"

Henry nodded.

"How would you like to have it? There are eighty acres of good land there."

Henry hesitated.

"There's some good timber on that land, Henry," his father reminded him.

All at once Henry knew what he wanted. The Moir farm was the answer.

"I'll take it," he said excitedly. "I'll set up a sawmill and cut off the timber. Then Clara and I can be married!"

Mr. Ford smiled contentedly. At last he had Henry settled on a farm. And Henry smiled contentedly, too, because at last he had found a way to marry Clara.

As soon as he could, Henry got a steam engine and set up a sawmill on the Moir farm. When winter came he began cutting trees and dragging the logs to his sawmill. Then he cut them into lumber. He saved some lumber to build a house and sold the rest in Detroit.

When the new house was finished, Henry and Clara moved in. Henry bought a new rug for the parlor, just like the one in his father's house. Clara liked the red roses and the fancy vases in the pattern. They made the organ she had brought from home look very grand.

As soon as they were settled, Henry made a workshop. As he was putting his tools in place, he thought of his road machine. He had had little time for it lately, for running the mill and building the house had taken all his time.

"It's still a good idea," he thought. "A machine like that could take most of the hard work out of farming."

Not long ago he had read an article about gasoline engines in a magazine. He had studied the article and the drawings with it carefully.

"I think I'll build a gasoline engine," he decided. "It can't be too much different from that engine I worked on a few years ago. I'll try a small one first."

He set to work at once. Within a few months

the engine was finished. It had one small cylinder and piston and a flywheel to make it run smoothly. But when he tried it out, it ran!

Henry was delighted. This was better than steam. It was just what he needed. Suddenly all his interest and enthusiasm returned.

"I'll have to learn more about these engines," he thought. "Not only that, I'll have to learn more about electricity, too. I'll have to use electricity to make the gasoline explode inside the cylinders in my engine."

Suddenly he grew more serious. "How can I learn about electricity here on the farm? The only place around here that has electricity is Detroit." He looked at his little engine again. Then he struck the workbench with his fist. "Clara won't like it," he thought, "but I just have to go back to Detroit!"

The Horseless Carriage

THE NEXT day Henry said, "I'm going to Detroit for a couple of days. I'll ask Margaret to come and keep you company."

Clara didn't suspect that this trip was different from the others Henry made to Detroit. "I think I'll ask James Ruddiman to come over to spend the evening, too," she said.

Henry laughed. "Clara, you're a born matchmaker. The first thing you know you'll have those two married. That would make you happy, wouldn't it?"

Laughing Clara waved him away and he started off to the city.

Detroit had changed since he had first gone there to work. The gas lights that had lighted the streets were gone and new electric lights had taken their places. All the stores and many of the homes were lighted by electricity, too. Woodward Avenue was paved with bricks and asphalt instead of cedar blocks. The horse-cars were gone. Electric streetcars rolled along the tracks in their places.

Just as he had known where he was going that other time, so today Henry went straight to the Edison Illuminating Company. Getting a job there was no problem. When the manager learned that he was a steam engineer, Henry was hired at once. The company needed a man to run the steam engines that made electricity.

"Looks as if I'll never get away from steam," Henry thought a little sadly. But he had a job in Detroit, and that was what he had wanted. Now he must break the news to Clara.

It took a whole day for him to get up enough courage to tell her what he had done. She knew he was excited about something, but she didn't ask questions.

That evening they sat in the parlor after supper. Henry's mind was filled with ideas. Now that he knew his gasoline engine would work he wanted to build a larger one. And when he had built it he wanted to build a light carriage to put it in. He knew just how it ought to be made. He could draw the plans right now.

"Clara," he said suddenly, "do you have some paper I could draw on?"

Without looking up from her knitting, Clara reached for a sheet of music on the organ and handed it to him. "Is this big enough?" she asked. "You can use the back of it."

Henry bent over the paper. For a while the click of Clara's needles and an occasional sigh from Henry were the only sounds in the room.

Suddenly Henry sprang to his feet. "Clara, I have it! There's my horseless carriage!"

Clara dropped her knitting needles in astonishment. "Your—what did you say, Henry?"

"Clara, you weren't listening to a word I said. I'm going to build a horseless carriage. Look, here it is." He handed her the drawing. "I'm going to make another gasoline engine, a larger one with two cylinders, and I'm going to put it in a light carriage. Then I can travel around the city and even out in the country if I want to."

Clara laughed. "A carriage without horses, Henry? When are you going to start?"

"I'm afraid you won't like this, Clara," he said uneasily. "We'll have to move to Detroit."

"Oh, Henry!" Clara's heart sank. "Do I have to leave my lovely new house?"

"I can't work on my horseless carriage here."

"Well, if you say so," she managed to say at last. "I know you can do anything you set your mind to. If you want to build a horseless carriage, you will."

THE RED BRICK SHED

So they moved to Detroit and Henry went to work for the Edison Illuminating Company as an engineer. At first they lived on John R Street, but later they moved into a little brick house on Bagley Avenue. It was not pretty like the house on the farm, but there were several things about it that Clara liked.

For one thing, it was close to Henry's work. For another, there was a little brick shed in back of the house, which Henry could use as a shop. "I don't want my kitchen cluttered up with a horseless carriage," Clara said. "I wouldn't be able to get any work done."

Henry laughed. "Well, the Fords made history today, Clara. They're the only family in

Detroit that have a shed for a carriage I'm carrying around in my head."

Since Henry worked at the Edison power plant at night, he had the early morning hours to spend in his shop. He fixed it up, then spent day after day designing and making parts for a two-cylinder engine. Sometimes a friend came in to help him, but much of the work he did himself. It was hard work, but satisfying.

At last the engine was finished, and he carried it proudly into the house. It was Christmas Eve. Clara was busy in the kitchen, getting ready for tomorrow.

"Henry, take that thing out of my kitchen!"

"I can't, Clara," he said excitedly. "It's finished, and I want to see whether it works."

"But not in here!"

"I have to try it here. I need electricity to make a spark in the cylinders, and there isn't any in the shed."

147

With a sigh, Clara cleared a place on the sink and Henry put the engine down.

"Now!" he said. "Will you pour the gasoline for me while I turn the flywheel? Only one drop at a time, mind you. Are you ready?"

He began to spin the wheel with his hands. There was a hesitant, sputtering cough, then another. Suddenly the coughs came faster and more regularly, and the flywheel began to turn by itself.

"It works!" Henry picked Clara up in his arms and swung her around. "Clara, it works!"

Test after test convinced Henry that he had built a good engine. Now all he had to do was build the carriage, and before long he would be trying it out on the street. He began collecting bicycle wheels, tires, pipe, chains, a carriage seat, nuts, bolts, wire and many other things.

"What are you going to call your carriage?" Clara asked one day.

148

"Well, Father would probably call it a fool contraption," Henry said. "But I'm going to call it a quadricycle."

At that moment there was a faint cry from the front of the house.

"Oh! We've wakened the baby!" Clara ran from the kitchen. Henry followed her to the bedroom and looked down at his new son, Edsel, lying in his crib.

"Poor little tyke," Clara said, bending over the crib. "What with your job at the power plant and your horseless carriage, he hasn't seen much of his daddy."

"I won't be working like this all the time," Henry said. "Wait till the quadricycle is finished. Still—" he thought a moment—"I like to work. I think it's fun, at least if I'm doing something I like. I don't mind the hours I've spent working on my quadricycle. I know it will be a big thing some day."

Clara picked up the baby. "You know, I'm glad you got that letter from Edsel before we gave the baby some other name."

"I was glad to hear from him. Edsel was always a good friend."

Edsel was a professor now. He taught in the school of pharmacy of a large university. As he had planned, he had learned to prepare medicines that would make people well. Now he was teaching what he had started to learn when he first sold herbs to Mr. Stearns.

CHIEF ENGINEER

A few days later, when Henry went to work, he was told that the manager wanted to see him. At first he was worried. "Have I done something wrong?" he wondered.

The manager soon set his mind at rest. "Henry," he said, "we've been looking for a new chief engineer. We've finally chosen you. Would you like the job?"

Henry beamed. "Who wouldn't like it?"

"It will mean a raise in salary, of course."

"That will please Clara," Henry thought. "She has been worried lately because the quadricycle has taken so much of our savings. That horseless carriage doesn't eat oats, but it certainly does eat plenty of money."

Henry hurried home after work to tell Clara the good news. She was pleased about the raise. But most of all she was pleased because the new job proved that Henry could do anything he put his mind to.

It Really Runs

IT WAS three o'clock in the morning. The city was fast asleep. Suddenly, without warning, the neighborhood around Bagley Avenue was awakened by a loud noise. It was the steady roar of a gasoline engine.

In the little brick shed behind the Ford house Henry and Clara were standing side by side, looking proudly at Henry's horseless carriage. It was Henry's engine that was making the noise. The carriage was finished and Henry had decided to try it out.

As the noise grew louder, lights appeared in the houses along the street. Then heads popped out of windows to see what the noise was about. In more than one house someone muttered something about "that idiot" Henry Ford.

Even if he could have heard them, Henry would not have cared. His horseless carriage was no longer just an idea in his head, but a moving, working machine.

"Henry," Clara said, "do you think you should try it now? It's raining outdoors. And besides, you'll waken the neighbors."

"We'll just take it around the block," Henry said. "I want to see whether it actually works."

Jim Bishop, one of the men who had been helping him, opened the door. Henry climbed into the seat and put his hands on the steering tiller or bar. "Well, here we go," he said. He headed for the door.

"Stop, Henry, stop!" Clara's voice was shrill with alarm.

But Henry didn't need her warning. He had

seen as soon as she had that his horseless carriage was wider than the door. Now that it was finished, he couldn't get it out of the shed!

"I'll fix that!" he cried. He sprang down, seized a hammer and started swinging at the door frame. Crash! Bang! Bricks and wood flew

until there was room enough for the quadricycle to leave the shed.

"Now!" Henry said with satisfaction. "Jim, you ride ahead on your bicycle to see whether the street is clear."

He pulled a lever and, with a roar of exhaust, the quadricycle moved into the alley.

When he returned some time later, Clara was waiting anxiously.

"It works, Clara!" he cried. "It works!"

"I knew it would." Her voice was calm, but she was just as excited as he. "I never had any doubt about it, Henry. Now you'll have to take it out and show it to your father. Why don't you go today? And be sure to tell me everything he says." She laughed. "I'd like to see his face when you drive up."

"When I go, I'm taking you and Edsel with me," Henry said.

"Do you think I'd better?" Clara asked. "Do

155

you think it would be all right for a lady to ride in it?"

"Clara, that's the silliest thing I've ever heard you say," Henry said. "We'll go next Sunday."

The following Sunday Henry drove down Bagley Avenue with Clara beside him, holding Edsel in her lap. They caused a great deal of excitement. Some people stared in amazement, some cheered, and others made fun of the strange carriage. But the noise of the engine frightened horses, and many drivers were angry.

When they reached the edge of the city Henry said, "We'd better stay on the back roads, I think. Many people will be out riding today."

Countless farm wagons had worn deep ruts in the back roads, however, and the carriage bounced up and down in them. Suddenly one wheel slipped into a deep hole and the steering tiller jerked to one side. Henry slowed down until he could get out of the hole. Then he straddled the rut, with two wheels bumping along the shoulder of the road and the other two riding the ridge in the center.

"They'll have to change the size of wagons, that's all there is to it," Henry said firmly. "Their wheels will have to be the same width as the wheels on horseless carriages."

As they rode along Henry talked endlessly, but Clara couldn't hear him over the noise of the engine. It didn't matter much. He was merely telling himself the changes he would make in the next quadricycle.

At last they came within sight of the farm. William was riding a bicycle around the barnyard. When he heard the noise of the engine, he looked up.

"Here comes Henry in his horseless carriage!" he shouted, running to the kitchen. "Come to the yard, everybody! Quick!"

By the time Henry had stopped in the driveway the whole family was standing around, staring at the carriage.

"Why, it really runs!" John cried as though he had made a great discovery. "It runs!"

Margaret swung Edsel off Clara's lap. "What was it like, Clara?" she asked eagerly.

"Henry will give you a ride. It's a wonderful carriage for a lady!" Clara said with a sly smile at Henry.

Henry was watching his father closely. Mr. Ford had not moved from his place near the back porch.

"Come on, Father," Henry said. "I'll ride you down the road a piece."

Mr. Ford gave Henry and the machine a cold look. "You couldn't hire me to ride in that fool contraption!" he said and stalked off to the barn.

Henry was disappointed.

Margaret put her hand on his arm. "Never mind, Henry. He'll be all right after a while."

158

"I didn't expect him to pat me on the back," Henry said. "But I didn't think he'd feel like that. What's wrong with him?"

"Maybe you can talk to him after dinner," Clara said.

"Well, who wants to go first?" Henry asked.

Everyone did.

"Ladies first," Henry decided, and helped Margaret into the seat.

One by one he took them all for a ride, back and forth out of the yard and down the road.

After dinner Henry did get a chance to talk to his father.

"What are you going to do with that thing now that you've wasted all this time on it?" Mr. Ford snapped scornfully.

"I'm going to build more like it," Henry answered eagerly. "I'm going to sell them."

"Who'd be stupid enough to buy a thing like that when he could buy a horse?"

Henry sighed. "What's the use?" he thought. "He'll never understand."

Suddenly Mr. Ford said, "If you go ahead and build more of these machines, what's going to happen to all the men who make buggies and wagons and harnesses?" He paused a moment, then added, "Not that I think it will happen."

"But can't you see, Father?" Henry said. "These machines are going to start a whole new industry. The men who make buggies now will learn to make engines and carriages like mine. New roads will be built. There will be more work for people than ever before."

Finally Mr. Ford smiled. "I've always said that a man has to do what he feels he has to do," he said. "I know it's true. But, Henry, why in heaven's name did you decide that you had to do something like this?"

"Henry," Clara put in, "don't you think we'd better start back before it grows dark?"

Henry stood up.

"Still," Mr. Ford went on with a deep sigh, "I guess once you've made your mind up to something, you're not likely to change it."

Margaret giggled. "As if you ever changed your mind, Father!"

The others laughed, but Mr. Ford looked puzzled.

"Have you all gone out of your minds?" he asked. "What are you laughing about?"

No one would tell him.

Soon Henry's horseless carriage became the talk of Detroit. Wherever he went, crowds gathered to look at it and to ask questions about it. If he left it alone for even a minute someone would try to drive it. He had to carry a chain and fasten the carriage to a lamp post whenever he left it.

Some people were interested in it, but most of them thought the carriage was a nuisance.

They said it made too much noise and frightened horses. The police didn't like it because it caused crowds to gather and block traffic. Finally Henry had to get permission from the mayor of the city to drive the machine on the streets.

Henry's boss disapproved of the quadricycle just as much as other people did. "I think you're on the wrong track," he said one day.

"What do you mean?" Henry asked shortly. He was growing tired of having people make fun of his carriage.

"Electricity's the thing, not gasoline," his boss replied. "You should know that. You're in the electric business. Thomas Edison ought to know, too. He's the greatest inventor in the world today."

"Well, of course he is," Henry answered. "But what does Edison have to do with my quadricycle anyway?"

"He has invented a thing which he calls a stor-

age battery. It produces an electric current. He has already run an electric train with batteries, and now he's putting them in small carriages like yours."

Henry's heart sank. "Have I wasted my time on gasoline engines?" he wondered. "Maybe I could have done better right here in the plant, trying to make an electric motor of some kind."

"I'd like to meet Thomas Edison," he said. "I'd like to ask him about those batteries."

"You probably will," replied his boss. "As chief engineer, you'll be going to a meeting in New York City soon. It's on developments in the electrical business, and Thomas Edison is going to be there."

Henry Finds
a Friend

On the first day of the meeting in New York, Henry tried all day to speak to Thomas Edison. But there were always so many important people with him that Henry could not get near. Finally, discouraged, Henry returned to his hotel and went to bed.

Early the next morning he went for a walk. A man came walking toward him briskly. He was breathing deeply of the fresh morning air. Henry smiled when he saw the man.

"There's another country boy," he thought. "I guess when you come from a farm you never lose the habit of getting up early."

When the man came closer, Henry recognized him. It was Thomas Edison! Henry tried to get up enough courage to speak, but he didn't have to worry. Mr. Edison spoke first.

Before long they were sitting together on a bench, talking eagerly. At last Henry had found a willing and interested listener.

He told Mr. Edison about his gasoline-powered carriage. He told him how he had built it and explained just how its internal combustion engine worked. Then, half fearfully, he mentioned Mr. Edison's electric car.

Thomas Edison laughed.

"You know, my boy, I just can't keep my fingers out of the electricity pie. Sometimes the pie's too hot and I have to lick my fingers. But if I couldn't experiment with electricity, life wouldn't be worth living.

"It made me happy to discover that a battery-powered car would work. I thought it was a great improvement over the steam engine. But it isn't practical. The batteries are too heavy for a small car. Besides, there aren't enough trained men in the country to keep the batteries charged and the cars in order."

Henry smiled with relief.

"Now I think you are on the right track," Mr.

Edison went on. "A self-moving car must be light and so simple that everyone can learn how to run it easily.

"Go on with your experiments, my boy. And, above all, don't be discouraged. There's nothing like trial and error to keep you on your toes. You'll never know how discouraged I was before that first electric light of mine lighted up."

"Thank you, Mr. Edison," Henry managed to say. He stood watching Edison go briskly down the sidewalk. "No wonder people call him the greatest inventor in the world," he thought. "He's the finest man I've ever met."

With Edison's encouragement, Henry went home determined to build another horseless carriage. He was going to make it better than the first one. While driving around Detroit and out to the farm and back, he had discovered many ways in which he could improve it.

One day he met the mayor of Detroit on the

street. His name was Maybury, and he was an old friend of the Ford family. Mr. Maybury wanted to know what Henry was doing with his quadricycle.

"I'm going to make another one," Henry said. "It will be much better than the last one."

"How will you improve it?" Mr. Maybury wanted to know.

Henry talked for an hour, and the mayor listened with interest.

"How long would it take you to build another machine?" he asked finally.

Henry's face fell. "Well, that's the trouble," he said. "A lot of time and hard work went into the first one. I made many of the parts by hand and, even so, it took most of my savings.

"If I had more money I could have some of the parts made," he went on. "There are many good machinists here in Detroit who could make them once they knew what I wanted. A carriage maker could make the body. That would save me a lot of time."

Mr. Maybury thought for a while. "How much money would you need to get started?" he wanted to know.

Henry gasped. "You mean you'll back me?"

"I'll get some other businessmen here in Detroit to help," Mr. Maybury said with a smile. "Now go to work. I want to see how soon you can get another car on the road."

Henry built his second car. It caused almost as much excitement as the first one. The improvements he had promised were to be seen in the car's changed appearance. There were fenders over the wheels, because Clara had complained when her dress was splattered with mud. The seat was larger so that Edsel could sit between them. The wheels were larger, and there was a new steering bar, better than the old one.

Mr. Maybury and his friends formed a company called the Detroit Automobile Company. Henry quit his job as chief engineer at the Edison Illuminating Company and became one of the officers in the new company. At last he was making automobiles.

That was what people were calling the horseless carriages now. The word came from the French language. *Auto* meant "self," and *mobile* meant "moving." And that was what Henry's horseless carriage was, self-moving.

The Detroit Automobile Company was not very successful. It made about twenty automobiles before it went out of business. Then Henry was out of a job.

By this time other companies were building automobiles, too. There were all kinds on the streets of Detroit now. Most of them were big and only the rich could buy them.

Henry was discouraged when the Detroit Automobile Company failed.

"Maybe Father is right after all," he told Clara. "Maybe we should go back to the farm. We're sure of a living there."

"Don't give up, Henry," Clara said. "You know you'd never be happy on the farm. You want to build automobiles."

"Yes, but who will back me now?"

"Build an automobile better and faster than any other. Then people will beg to help."

Henry thought for a moment. Suddenly he smiled. "You always were my Great Believer," he said. "You've always encouraged me when things looked worst. And now you've given me the very idea I needed. I'll build a racer."

"A racer!"

"Yes," Henry said excitedly. "You know, everyone's talking about Alexander Winton's new racer, the 'Bullet.' If I could build a car that would beat the 'Bullet' I wouldn't have any trouble starting another company."

Henry set to work immediately and designed and built a racer. When it was finished he raced it against the 'Bullet' and won. Everyone talked about him and said that he was the best designer of automobiles in the country. Now he had no trouble at all getting his old backers to set him up in business again. This time they named their company the Henry Ford Company.

First of all Henry designed and started to build another racer. It was a powerful car. The roar of its engine at full speed was deafening. Henry was determined to make this car go faster than any car had gone before.

His backers were more interested in making a passenger car. Soon they began to quarrel with Henry and he finally left the company, taking the racer with him.

In the race against Alexander Winton, Henry himself had raced. But he did not care to race his new car, which he called "999."

"You'd better get someone who knows how to race," one of his helpers said one day.

"Who?" asked Henry. "I don't know anyone."

"There's a bicycle racer out west named Barney Oldfield. Let me send for him. I think he might be interested."

Barney Oldfield had never driven an automobile before. In a few days Henry and one of his assistants taught him how to handle the car. Henry fitted it with a big two-handled tiller, or steering bar, so that Barney could hold the machine on the track with both hands. Then Barney practiced for a few days.

At last the day of the race came. Alexander Winton was there again, along with several other famous drivers. The cars were lined up and their engines were started. At the starting signal, Barney Oldfield leaped forward with an ear-splitting roar and took the lead. He roared down the track and around the first turn at full speed

and never let up until the race ended. By that time he had passed every other car in the race at least once.

Henry Ford's name appeared in all the newspapers. He was well known now and had no trouble finding men who wanted to put money in another company. This time the company was to be known as the Ford Motor Company.

The first car Henry designed for the new company he called the Model A. It was similar to his other cars, but had many improvements. It had a steering wheel instead of a tiller, and two seats instead of one. There were many smaller changes, too.

People liked the Model A, and the new company prospered. But some of his partners wanted to build expensive cars, as the other automobile companies did.

"I don't want to build big cars," Henry said. "Let the others build them. I want to build a small, inexpensive car which everybody can buy, not just the wealthy."

He went on, year after year, designing smaller and lighter cars. Each new model was named with a letter of the alphabet. When he reached the Model N he called it a runabout. It was his first four-cylindered car. It was small and light and useful. People liked it and bought it by the thousands. Now Henry was sure that he was on the right track. He would build a car that everyone could own.

THE MODEL T

At first he carried his ideas around in his head. Then, bit by bit, his ideas were put into shape. He spent hours and days in the factory, watching the parts being made, giving encouragement or making suggestions to the workmen. Soon the men caught his excitement, too, and did their

177

best to make the new car just exactly as he wanted it.

At last Henry was satisfied, and the Ford Motor Company brought out the new car, which was called the Model T. It was an immediate success everywhere, and orders came in faster than the factory could fill them.

In order to take care of the increased business, the company built a new factory in Highland Park, a suburb of Detroit. When it was completed, this was the largest automobile factory in the world. Even so, it could not make automobiles fast enough to meet the demand. The company still fell behind in filling orders.

"Well," Henry said, "we'll just have to find ways to build cars faster." He set men to work designing new machines which would make the parts faster and more cheaply. But even these machines could not produce parts fast enough to meet the demand for the Model T.

Then Henry said, "Let's bring the work to the men instead of having them go to the work."

Endless conveyor belts and lines were built to bring the parts to a main assembly line. Each worker on the assembly line added the part that came to him. Then the car moved down the line to the next man, who added something else. As it passed each man, the car grew larger and more complete until, at the end of the line, a finished Model T stood ready to drive away.

The assembly lines helped the company to make many more cars. But still more people wanted to buy Model T's, and still more people were needed to make them. As Henry had once said they would, carriage makers learned how to make bodies, and small machine shops grew into large factories supplying parts for the Model T.

The new factory turned out so many cars that there was no place to store them. Trains hauled them away from the factory as quickly as possi-

the wages he had been receiving before. As a result, thousands of people came to Detroit in search of work.

Soon a Ford factory was built in Canada and another one in England. Before long Henry Ford's name and the Model T were familiar to the whole world. It was a new and different world, which Henry himself had put on wheels.

Henry had never given up his dream of building a machine that would make farm work easier. Now he began to work on a tractor. At the same time he began to plan a new factory, for the Highland Park plant was already too small.

When Henry told his partners that he wanted to use the company's profits to develop the tractor and build the new plant, they objected.

One by one, Henry bought them out. Finally

181

only he and Edsel owned stock in the Ford Motor Company. Edsel, who had been working in the plant for some time, became president.

Then Henry began his new factory. He owned land along the Rouge River, near Dearborn, and used a thousand acres of it for his Rouge River plant. This factory was to become just as famous as the Model T itself.

When the plant was finished, he made the Rouge River deep enough for boats. Then he bought boats and built docks for them. The boats brought steel, coal, iron ore and other raw materials to the factory.

An underground tunnel from the Detroit River brought water to the factory. Henry built a power plant to provide his own electricity. The Rouge River factory was the finest in the world and remained the finest for many years to come.

In 1927 the last Model T rolled off the assembly line at the old Highland Park plant. Since Henry had first designed it, fifteen million Model T's had been sold throughout the world.

Henry was unhappy when he stopped making the Model T. To him it was still the finest car in the world, but people wanted something fancier now. He and his engineers designed another car to take the Model T's place. He called it the Model A.

As he stood in his huge Rouge River plant

looking at the first Model A, Henry grew thoughtful. "It has been a long time since I designed the first Model A," he thought. "The world has certainly changed since then."

He could have said, "Henry Ford has certainly changed the world since then." For he had made the automobile a necessary part of the American way of life. He had almost changed the face of the country by causing countless highways to be built across it. And, in doing so, he had also become one of the wealthiest men in the new world that he had helped to bring into being.

What was it his father had said once?

"Yes, once Henry makes up his mind to something, he isn't likely to change it."

Greenfield Village

THERE is a little village within the city of Dearborn, Michigan, not far from Detroit. Some people call it a "village of living history." Its real name is Greenfield Village.

People do not live in the houses in Greenfield Village, but visitors may go there and walk through the houses. They watch men at work in the different shops and can even buy candy in the general store.

Henry Ford was the founder of Greenfield Village. He wanted to keep alive, for the coming generations, the history of the America he knew.

The village is more than a living history of

185

Henry Ford's boyhood. It is the living history of yesterday in America. Henry Ford's boyhood was part of that yesterday.

Along the streets of the village are buildings and scenes, as they were in the past. There are the actual houses, schools, and stores where Henry Ford lived, worked, and played.

There is the Scotch Settlement School, with the teacher's platform, the wood-burning stove, and the water bucket and dipper standing in the corner. The desk in the last seat of the first row has the initials H F and E A R carved on its top, just as Henry and Edsel carved them many years ago.

There is a white farmhouse with a white picket fence running around the yard. It is the original Ford farmhouse. In the kitchen a clock stands on a shelf, the first timepiece that Henry could remember. There is the stove that stood in his father's kitchen. It was on this stove that

Henry put the teakettle with a copper whistle in its spout and turned Margaret's tears to smiles.

One day, when Henry had almost completely restored the farmhouse of his boyhood, Margaret held her hands behind her back and said, "Which hand do you take?"

Henry laughed when he remembered the game they used to play. "The right one," he said.

Margaret opened her hand, and there was the little copper whistle, Henry's good-luck piece that he thought he had lost long ago.

He put it in a place of honor on his workbench under the east window in the dining room. The tools he had made to repair the watch Mike gave him are there, too. There is a screwdriver made from a nail, tweezers made from a corset stay, and a punch made from a knitting needle.

Farther along in the village stands Miller School, rebuilt just as Henry remembered it. There is a well with a bucket hanging from a rope on the windlass. In front of the school a paddle wheel, like the paddle wheels Henry built in Roulo Creek, turns in a little stream.

Down the street is McGill's Jewelry Store. In the back room is the workbench where Henry had to hide to repair watches for Mr. McGill.

Of course the red brick shed from Bagley Avenue is there, the little shed in which the first horseless carriage was made. It was moved on runners from Detroit to Greenfield Village. Inside, Henry's old tools are lined up on the workbench. The quadricycle, which wakened his neighbors in the middle of the night, is there, too.

Henry went to Connecticut to find an apothecary shop that looked like Mr. Stearns's shop. There are bottles of drugs and old-fashioned tonics on the shelves. Back of the wood stove is a case of drawers filled with herbs, such as fennel, tansy and others that Edsel Ruddiman collected for Mr. Stearns.

Near by stands the Edison Illuminating plant, where Henry used to work. He bought the building and its machinery and had them all moved to Greenfield Village.

Overlooking the village green stands a little church. It is the Martha-Mary Chapel, named for Henry's mother, Mary, and Clara's mother, Martha. There are bricks in this building that came from Clara's home in Greenfield, the name he gave his village. Each weekday morning services are held in the Chapel by the children of the Greenfield Village schools. It is a great honor to be chosen to attend the Greenfield schools. Henry Ford wanted children to "learn by doing."

Henry Ford collected buildings as other people might collect stamps or coins. Each building and everything in it helped to tell the story of America as it was in the early 1900's.

Everyone was curious about a large tract of

189

land that he left untouched. "What are you going to put there?" they asked him.

Henry merely smiled. "That's going to be used to honor my closest friend," he said.

Everyone knew who that was—Thomas Edison, America's great scientist and inventor.

To honor Edison, Henry bought the old laboratory at Menlo Park, where Edison had made

190

the first electric light. He had the buildings taken apart and shipped to Dearborn. Edison had worked on many other inventions there, too, such as the phonograph, the moving picture camera, and the first electric railway in the United States.

Henry Ford rebuilt or reproduced every building that Edison had worked in. He built a white picket fence around them. He even had red New Jersey soil brought to Dearborn to complete the picture.

When people learned that Henry Ford was collecting "antiques" they started to send him things from all over the world. They sent everything from flatirons to baby buggies. From the beginning, he had planned to build a museum where every automobile that he or the Ford Motor Company had made could be displayed. By the time his building was completed, he had enough antiques to tell another story of America.

It takes all day to visit every collection in the Ford Museum. The story of farm machinery from hand plows to tractors is shown. Carriages, automobiles, trains, and streetcars show the changes in transportation. The display of things for the home shows the wonderful progress that has been made.

Not far away automobiles and trucks speed past over eight-lane superhighways. Across the road is the Research and Experimental Center of the Ford Motor Company, alive with activity. In near-by fields farm tractors move round and round on their endless task of cultivating the soil. Overhead a jet-propelled airplane streaks across the sky.

It was all started here, in the simple unhurried days of the past, by Henry Ford, the boy from Dearborn, the boy with ideas.